UNLEASHED

TRICK OR TRUTH

Ali Sparkes
UNLEASHED
TRICK OR TRUTH

OXFORD
UNIVERSITY PRESS

OXFORD
UNIVERSITY PRESS

Great Clarendon Street, Oxford OX2 6DP

Oxford University Press is a department of the University of Oxford.
It furthers the University's objective of excellence in research, scholarship,
and education by publishing worldwide in

Oxford   New York

Auckland   Cape Town   Dar es Salaam   Hong Kong   Karachi
Kuala Lumpur   Madrid   Melbourne   Mexico City   Nairobi
New Delhi   Shanghai   Taipei   Toronto

With offices in

Argentina   Austria   Brazil   Chile   Czech Republic   France   Greece
Guatemala   Hungary   Italy   Japan   Poland   Portugal   Singapore
South Korea   Switzerland   Thailand   Turkey   Ukraine   Vietnam

Oxford is a registered trade mark of Oxford University Press
in the UK and in certain other countries

British Library Cataloguing in Publication Data

Data available

ISBN: 978-0-19-275608-4

1 3 5 7 9 10 8 6 4 2

Printed in Great Britain

Paper used in the production of this book is a natural,
recyclable product made from wood grown in sustainable forests.
The manufacturing process conforms to the environmental
regulations of the country of origin.

**For Charlie
Patey**

With grateful thanks to illusion and
performance genius Peter Clifford for his
expert guidance on all things magical.

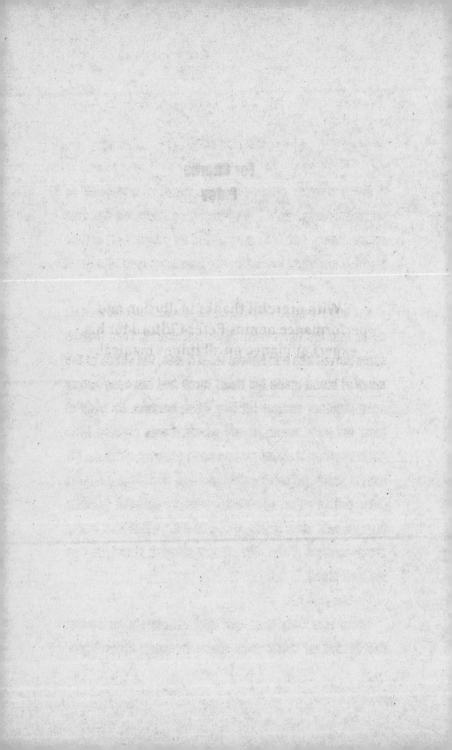

Collecting

A warm spatter down his face brought him back to consciousness. No . . . *up* his face. Because he was upside down. Painfully suspended by a tight belt across his hips and right shoulder, his knees jammed, his arms flung up . . . no . . . down.

The warm spatter trickled up his cheek and followed its curve into the outer dent of his left nostril. Even though some part of him had known what it was, the shock of the *smell* of blood made his heart lurch and his eyes spring open. Another spatter hit him. Then another. He tried to twist his head round to see where it was coming from but his knees, wedged fast, were in the way, blocking his line of sight. He realized he was not completely upside down but on a kind of oblique angle, or else the dripping blood would have hit his knees, not his head. And it was dropping from a distance. It had velocity. It couldn't be his own blood.

Whose was it?

There was only dim light and absolutely no sound. Odd planes of colour and shape wrapped around him.

His brain could not make sense of any of them. When he opened his mouth and tried to make some noise he couldn't hear anything at all. The only certainty came with another small warm splash. More blood. Not his. Whose?

His mind grasped, fumbling like a drunk, for something else. *I am Spook Williams,* he told himself. *I am . . . important. I am . . . a Cola.*

A sudden burst of cinema went off deep in his brain—throwing up a series of scenes at lightning speed, like the trailer for a high-octane movie. He was at Fenton Lodge, his college . . . eating breakfast this morning . . . Lisa and Gideon and Dax were there. Now outside by the steps—and there was Mia, tall, dark, distant—but with a warmth that he could never fathom, giving him a little wave. His insides clenched a little at the thought of Mia. What if this blood was *hers*?

Because somewhere even deeper in his brain he was certain that the red drops raining gently upon him came from someone he cared about.

There was a lurch. Wherever he hung, suspended and helpless, it was on the move. He felt rather than heard the crunch of metal, the splinter of glass, and his knees finally began to tip further sideways. Pain shot through his left wrist and with it came a sudden crash of audio. A scream and a rhythmic thudding. Spook Williams's eyes opened and saw someone dangling above him. Someone with a gash across his forehead; eyes shut, mouth slack, showering blood on his best friend.

Spook felt horror beat at his throat. He heard the scream again and realized it was his own. '*DARREN! DARREN! DA*—'

1

'—rren? Darren! Wake up, you lazy oaf!'

Darren Tyler rolled over in bed and groaned at
Spook. His mousy hair was stuck up on one side and
his grey eyes crinkled up as he realized what day it
was. He settled heavily onto his back and yawned
deeply at the high ceiling of their dorm. Spook was
dressed already and had pulled back the thick blue
curtains, letting light spill through the windows,
which were high and mullioned with many old
glass panes. They let a *lot* of light through.

'Spook—where *did* you learn to speak like that?'
enquired Darren.

'Like what?'

'Like a medieval baron,' said Darren. 'Lazy *oaf*?'

Spook smirked. 'I'm descended from royalty,
didn't you know? On my father's side.'

5

'Ah yes,' grinned Darren. 'I nearly forgot.' He sat up and kicked off the quilt. 'All ready for bone-cracking fun, then, your lordship?'

'I don't see why Mia can't mend you,' said Spook, checking his reflection in the tall mirror above the oak dresser. He thumbed a penny sized nugget of white wax out of a pot and worked it around his palms before running his long fingers through his close cropped hair. It was dark red, thick and slightly wavy. Spook was obsessed with keeping it under control.

'Because I don't want her to,' said Darren. 'And neither does Mrs Sartre.'

'She healed my broken ankle,' said Spook, and his eyes, in the mirror, took on a misty look that Darren could see even from his bed.

'Yep—and would you let her heal it again? If you could get it sorted in the usual way? Knowing what you know now?'

Spook turned to stare at Darren. Sometimes his friend was annoyingly on the ball, for a dozy little half baked glamourist. Mia *had* healed his ankle four years ago and saved him from considerable agony. He'd been very grateful at the time. Of all the other Children Of Limitless Ability who'd been found by the government and brought together to be educated—and monitored—in secret, Spook couldn't rate one more highly than Mia. She was a healer of extraordinary talent even back then, when she was just twelve. Now, at sixteen, she was . . . well, Darren would probably say 'awesome'—but Spook didn't go in for such Americanisms.

'No. No, I wouldn't now,' he acknowledged. 'I can take my own pain.'

They had discovered that first year that Mia did not know how to release the pain she was taking from others. She'd very nearly killed herself. She'd later learned techniques to safely release the pain she took—but Spook still felt a belt of guilt when he thought of that roadside healing. He hadn't known then, though. Nobody had. And guilt wasn't a feeling Spook bothered with too much. It served no purpose.

'Anyway—it gets us out, doesn't it?' Darren was saying, stomping across to grab his robe. 'All the way to West Cumberland Hospital for specialist treatment to sort my wonky knee out for good! It'll be a laugh.'

Spook shook his head and snorted. 'Only a Cola would say that. Only a Cola would see a day trip to get his bones skewered as a thrill. We really need to get out more.'

'Be grateful for what you can get,' said Darren, disappearing off to the shower room.

Spook pulled on some fine black leather boots which tapered to a squared off point at the toe. He didn't follow the obsession with trainers that every other student here had. He liked to look . . . sleek . . . dark . . . mysterious. And so he was. He did wear jeans—but only black ones with excellent cut and fit. Today's shirt was indigo blue which set off the amber tones in his eyes. He really did have *the look* . . . even if he did say so himself. His face was narrow with well defined jaw and cheekbones and his eyes were fringed with lashes of dark auburn . . . not that pale blond-y look which many redheads got saddled with. If he'd got *that* he might have had to resort to dyeing them. He'd also got lucky on the freckle front—just a very fine sprinkling across his straight nose—not that pebble-dashed effect that less fortunate gingers had to cope with.

No. He was a very good specimen and rarely got teased for his hair colour. Of course, that could also be something to do with being the best illusionist on the planet. If anyone dared to make fun of him they paid for it. Spook could make them see quite horrific things. Illusions so detailed and so pulsatingly real that they briefly forgot that they *were* illusions. Sometimes they even screamed.

'D'you think it'll hurt much?' Darren came back into the room after very possibly the shortest shower in his personal history.

'What, putting one of your legs in a metal cage and drilling four bits of rusty steel into it? No! Why would it?' Spook arched an eyebrow.

'Why exactly *am* I your friend?' said Darren, getting dressed with as little care and attention as possible.

'Because I inspire you to be better,' said Spook, sitting down to check his silk-and-wool-mix black socks were smooth and evenly positioned above his ankles. 'And to get your lazy arse out of bed on time. They'll stop serving breakfast in ten minutes.'

A small green figure bounced onto his knee, turned its back and pulled down its trousers, giving Spook the benefit of two fluffy rounded buttocks. A dainty purple cloud of what he assumed was meant to be a fart rose from them. Then the creature broke up like a poor satellite feed.

'Hmmm—hard to see,' said Spook. 'As transparent

as usual . . . and no audio at all. A three out of ten, I'd say, but I can tell that your illusory wit is improving every day. With this kind of repartee you'll be rivalling Oscar Wilde!'

Darren merely laughed and supplied the fart noise for real. 'And I don't *need* to hurry to breakfast,' he said, opening their dorm door. 'I can't eat anything, remember? Operation? Nil by mouth since last night.'

'Well, you can watch me do what you can't then,' said Spook, walking past him with a smirk. 'you're used to that.'

Darren rolled his eyes. 'Again . . . note to self. Why *is* Spook Williams my friend?'

Breakfast was hurried. Only Gideon, Lisa and Dax were left, loitering over tea and toast at one end of the table, discussing Luke's speech patterns.

Spook collected a bowl of porridge and sprinkled it liberally with soft brown sugar before sitting at the other end of the table. Darren got some peppermint tea, and sipped it without much satisfaction, not saying much, trying not to think about his upcoming surgery. Spook had no choice but to listen in to the conversation between Gideon, Lisa and Dax.

'I heard him again last night,' said Gideon. 'On the way to the showers. He said "Damn! Forgot the shampoo!".'

'Did he really?' said Dax, grinning as if Luke was a toddler who'd just started reciting Shakespeare. Luke was sixteen, for pity's sake. What was the big deal? Just because Gideon's twin brother had been mute for a few months after a bit of trauma in France. Spook felt his lip rise in a sneer. He really couldn't help it. He was surrounded by idiots.

'It's so weird, the way it just comes out of the blue,' went on Gideon. 'And so . . . brilliant after all this time. I just wish he could, you know . . . talk more.'

'Gideon,' sighed Spook, reaching languidly for the teapot. 'You talk easily enough for half a dozen mute Reader brothers. Why don't you just leave Luke to his meaningful silences?'

Of course, all three glared at him as if he'd just shot their dog. They never could get a joke.

'Well,' said Gideon, swiping the teapot out of Spook's hands without leaving his seat and sending it high into the air on a telekinetic pulse. 'For someone who's had his life saved at least *twice* by a Reader brother, you really should appreciate ANY noise either of us makes.'

Spook sighed and tried to ignore the showing off. The teapot was poised above his head, ready to splash boiling beverage on him at any second. He forced himself to continue eating his porridge and with a wave of one hand sent an illusion shimmying down the carpet past the cutlery table. Lisa squawked and slapped her hand over her mouth, trying to stifle her giggles. Spook was delighted to see Gideon's face go pink.

Gideon's phantom double was now performing a cancan, wearing nothing but an ill-fitting pink bikini and high-heeled sandals and swinging a sequinny handbag. Lisa was now in fits. Even Dax was gripping her shoulder and trying to get a faint image. As a shapeshifter, who spent a lot of time in animal form, he was the only Cola known to be resistant to glamour and could never see the illusions Spook conjured. He could catch a vague impression of them, though, sometimes— if in physical contact with someone else who was witnessing the spectacle. 'What is it, Lees?' he was asking, fascinated.

'Cut it OUT, Williams!' snapped Gideon and the teapot shook threateningly.

'Pour me some tea and I will,' said Spook, calmly

spooning up more porridge and getting bikini-Gideon to do the splits while blowing kisses. Darren was also guffawing by now and Gideon, gritting his teeth, swiftly set down the teapot with a judder. A slop of escaped brown liquid shot from its spout and arced into Spook's mug. Spook ended the illusion.

'Later,' said Gideon, pointing at him. 'Just . . . later.'

'Come on. Let's find Mia and see if she can persuade Luke to say a few words,' said Lisa. The three got up and walked out, but Lisa paused at the door, sweeping her long blonde hair up into a scrunchy, and stared back at Spook.

'Oooh! Big sharp pain coming, Spook!' she said, achieving the ponytail and letting it swing down.

'You really think Gideon can land one on *me*?' said Spook. 'I'd like to see him try without using tele power. Now *that* would impress me.'

Lisa's eyes went a bit fluttery, as they often did when some psychic or spirit message was coming through. 'Through a joint. Sharp pain. Nasty!'

'Um . . .' Darren put down his peppermint tea and looked slightly queasy. 'That would be *me*, Lisa! Remember—knee operation today? Thanks for reminding me how much it'll hurt. Nice one.'

Lisa's eyes refocused. She shrugged. 'Sorry, Darren. Thought it was for the Great Self-Obsessedo next to you. You shouldn't sit so close to him. You might catch Git Disease.'

She went to go after Dax and Gideon, but then stopped again, twisting round and grabbing the door frame as if to stop herself falling. She looked confused and her dark blue eyes were fixed, staring back into the room at nothing. 'Collector's coming,' she said, sounding deeply surprised. '*Very* blue . . . Which way do you go? Get ready to choose.'

Spook felt goose pimples rise on his arms and across his neck. Darren was frozen, staring at Lisa.

'Oi! Get a move on, Hardman!' bellowed Gideon from somewhere in the hallway.

Lisa suddenly snapped back to reality. 'Good luck today, Darren. Sorry you're going to have the Great Self-Obsessedo holding your hand!'

And then she was gone.

'What was *that* about?' asked Darren. 'Get ready to choose? Choose what?'

'Darren, how many times do you have to watch Lisa Hardman wind you up before you realize she's just messing with your mind?' said Spook.

14

'Well,' said Darren, with a nervous click in his voice. 'She's right sometimes . . . quite a lot right . . .'

'Yes, well, I dare say you'll get to choose between pink or blue knee bolts today,' smiled Spook, getting to his feet. 'Come on. The coach will be waiting now. To say nothing of the SAS nannies. Welcome to another jolly Cola day out . . .'

Collecting

Darren didn't reply. He hung limply, suspended by his seatbelt, his eyes half closed and his mouth dripping blood. Spook called again, struggling to be free of his own seat belt and the buckled-up seats behind and in front of him. That was when the pain in his wrist went off like a bomb blast and his cries for Darren turned into a shriek of horror.

Pain seemed to brighten all his senses because now he could see properly—which wasn't necessarily a good thing. He could see his left wrist. He could also see the thin rod of metal, burst from the wrecked coach seat, which had skewered right through it. He could see the puffy purple bloom as blood escaped riotously under the pierced skin. On the exit side of the wound it was running down the rod in fast beads like a crimson water feature.

Where were the soldiers? What the hell was going on?

Only minutes ago he and Darren had been slouched in their seats, stretched out on doubles on either side of the aisle in the small coach, talking about Jennifer Troke, the glamourist Darren fancied. The coach was a state-of-the-art armoured vehicle with two armed SAS soldiers inside with them and a third driving—it was more like a prisoner relocation than a day out to a hospital. Spook had seriously expected an RAF helicopter to be tracking them a thousand feet above the winding Cumbrian road—but it seemed the Cola Project had relaxed a bit on that count. Charged with protecting and nurturing more than a hundred Children Of Limitless Ability (and limitlessly useful to their country, Spook never forgot) the Cola Project possessed the very best of the most cutting edge surveillance equipment for short- and long-range threat; clearly nobody was expecting any attack today.

So what had *happened*? Spook called out again, through gritted teeth, trying not to whimper like a girl, in spite of the worst pain he'd ever felt. Nobody responded. Were the soldiers dead? Was *Darren*? What had caused the crash?

RUMBLE . . . His brain now threw up some more images. He'd been glancing out of the window—well, checking his reflection in it, if he was honest—when the first *RUMBLE* caught his attention. Rocks. There were rocks rumbling down the steep fell to the left of the road. An avalanche! High up. So high, he thought, as his brain calculated the odds of danger—swiftly and inaccurately—that they

18

might drive on out of its path in time.

He had heard one of the SAS nannies shout a warning and a responding shout from the driver, even through the bullet-proof glass divide. He hadn't had time to look back at Darren and warn him before the shattering crash. Then the coach was swerving and rolling, brakes screaming, ceiling buckling under the raining rock. And then they were rolling . . . and rolling . . . bodies jarring brutally as gravity and velocity snatched at them and forced them into war with their seat belts. How long this had gone on Spook didn't know. He'd been unconscious when the vehicle came to rest.

'Please . . . someone . . .' whimpered Spook, no longer caring about how he sounded; only that there was someone still to hear him. His wrist felt as if it were being endlessly electrocuted.

Someone came. Nobody he was expecting. But as the pain went swiftly away, Spook really didn't care.

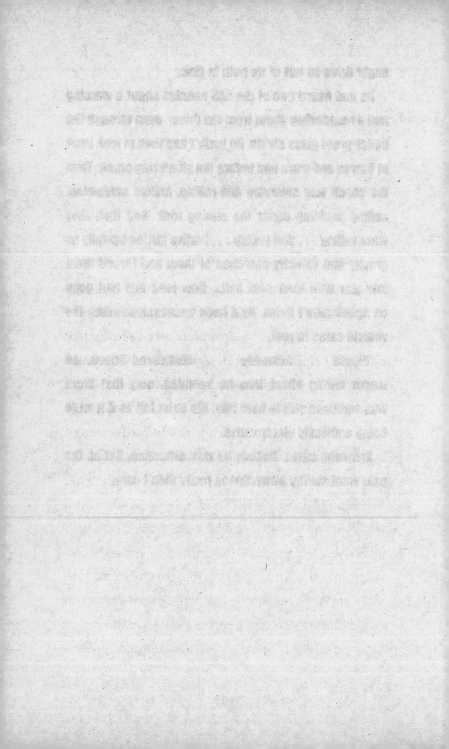

2

He awoke in a vast bed. A bed so wide and long that he could do a complete 'mattress angel' in it and not feel the edges. The duvet was silky smooth, like satin, and rippled weightlessly as his moving limbs disturbed it. The pillows were satin too, and white. He decided he was probably dreaming. Except for the insistent press on his bladder. He badly needed to urinate. But that could be in the dream too . . .

He gazed around the room, rather hoping the dream would last a while longer, because this room was right up his street. The walls were lined with milk-coloured suede and trimmed with dark wood skirting and cornices. Soft spotlights were set into more suede panels in the low ceiling above him. On either side of the vast bed were dark wood drawer units and each had a broad-brimmed golden

21

parchment lampshade set on a heavy bronze base. The lamps were switched on, adding more golden light to the room.

A shallow glass bowl of red lilies rested on a long low blanket box, of the same dark wood, at the foot of the bed. And off to the right, in a window alcove, was a blue suede two-seater sofa. The three windows above it were round. Folded on the sofa were clothes. Even from this distance Spook could tell that these were also right up his street. Dark turquoise chinos, expensively cut and sleek. A skinny-rib black T-shirt in gleaming fabric, fresh from some opulent store.

This was a *good* dream.

I'll stay here for as long as possible, thought Spook. Because he knew that what was happening in his waking life was not good. Really not good. Involving shock and pain and possibly grief. This dream was a far better place to be, even if he *could* feel some of that pain, seeping in through the fragile membrane of this dream world, from that real world beyond. His wrist twinged. A flash of memory tried for him—*metal*—*blood*—but he pushed it away and went on looking around the room, trying hard also to ignore the nagging need to pee.

He could smell leather—fine leather, probably Italian. And something cooking somewhere. And the heady scent of the red lilies. Beneath all this, though, was a steady, pervasive fragrance; something he knew well. Fresh, mineral, familiar. It took only the gentle sway of the room that his inner ears were now registering for it to fall into place. The sea. He was at *sea*! In a beautiful, beautiful boat.

Spook sprang up into sitting position and then yelped as a crack of pain registered through his wrist. *Metal! Blood!* The image of his skewered skin shuddered through his mind. DAMN! Now the dream would end and he would wake up back in the coach wreck. DAMN!

He took some steadying breaths, his eyes closed tight, and readied himself for the onslaught of that grim reality from which he'd just been enjoying temporary relief. After a few moments, though, he could still feel the satin across his legs; still smell the lilies, the leather, the cooking, and the sea. He opened his eyes again, his heart thumping. Where the hell *was* he?

As glad as he was not to return to the crash, he was now seriously freaked out. This was no hospital. It was certainly no part of Fenton Lodge. As nice as the dorms were (and he and Darren, privileged as two of the True Eleven, shared one of the best)—this was something *else*.

How had he got here? And when? How long ago? He stared down at his left wrist and saw that it was set in a neat, small cast; sparkling white plaster of Paris holding the no doubt wrecked bones inside immobile. The pain he'd experienced was from the sudden movement of his hand against the cast. It hurt, yes, but barely registered on the scale of pain he'd known in the crash. So . . . He must have been here a while . . . a day? Maybe two? Instinctively he raised his right hand to his chin and upper lip and felt a little soft stubble. Try as he might, growing any kind of stubble took time and what did grow was hardly visible. He barely needed to shave more than once or twice a week—but he *had shaved* on the morning he and Darren had been in the crash. So . . .

Darren. Another thud shook his chest. What had happened to his friend? Darren might not be the best illusionist in the world (how could he be, alongside Spook Williams?) and his bathroom habits left much to be desired . . . but he was the only friend Spook had. That meant something. Was he OK? Or . . . was he . . . *not*?

His legs felt shaky when he tested them, placing his bare feet on the thick cream carpet. He pressed his toes deep into the pile, noting with some relief that he was wearing boxer shorts. None that he recognized, mind you. Dark blue silk. He tried not to think of how they'd got there. If this *wasn't* a dream. And he still hadn't decided about that.

A door was ajar in the left corner of the room, emitting a pale light and a glimmer of pearly tiled wall. He made for it. Inside was a sumptuous bathroom with a circular jacuzzi tub set low into the thickly carpeted floor, a shower in a clear glass tube, echoing the circle of the bath, a circular glass basin beneath a circular mirror and next to this, a circular toilet. Spook lifted its round glass lid and sighed with relief a few seconds later.

Next he splashed water on his face, awkwardly, with one hand, noting a pale bruise on his right cheekbone. Otherwise he looked normal. He found a toothbrush and toothpaste—both clearly unused—and deployed them across his mouth before returning to the cabin.

He walked carefully across to the sofa and stared through the middle porthole. A silver line stretched across the lower half—the handrail of a walkway just outside—and beyond that the deep, fathomless blue of some ocean. Which ocean? Something in its colour and the soft roll of the waves made him doubt it was the North Sea.

Gulping down his fear, which was becoming insistent in the pit of his belly, now that the distracting call of his bladder was settled, Spook picked up the dark turquoise chinos and put them on. They fitted him perfectly; a rare thing for someone so tall and lean. As if they'd been tailored for him. He noticed a belt—a thick weave of golden suede strips and jade wool—and looped it through, doing the bronze clasp up with a satisfying click. The black T-shirt slid on luxuriously. Glancing down he saw no socks, but some black canvas deck shoes with coiled rope soles. He smiled and shook his head without much surprise when he discovered these were a perfect fit too.

Dressed, he felt stronger, although the weakness in his limbs suggested it was a long time since he'd eaten. His stomach gurgled as he took in another lungful of the cooking scent. It smelt like a barbecue . . . roasting steak and onions and peppers. His mouth watered. But all of this was fighting with the deepening sense of panic about where he was. It was time to find out.

He half expected the door to be locked, but although the shining chrome handle was heavy and the door itself weightier still, it opened easily enough. He pulled it wide and stepped over the dark wood and chrome ridge which rose six inches up from the carpet at the base of the door.

His deck shoe landed on a highly polished wooden walkway, perhaps a metre wide, and a salt-scented breeze ruffled his hair. He grasped the steel rail in front of him, watching the intensely blue water rippling two metres below. He could surely *not* be dreaming this—not with so many senses firing. And now, as if to convince him, his hearing joined in. In the room it had been incredibly quiet, damped by the suede and the satin and the thick carpet. Now he could hear the gentle sigh of the calm sea and the occasional splash against the anchored hull; the breeze passing his face and . . . voices . . . above him. Not far away. His heart lurched. He drew in another steadying breath. It was time to meet some people.

Steps led up to his left. He grabbed the polished chrome rail and followed its tight turn up to the next deck. Arriving on another walkway similar to the one he'd just left, his ears told him the laughter and talk was coming from another level up. He climbed the next curving set of steps, noting the glistening woodwork under his feet; the flawless white of the polished fibreglass beneath the rail; the smell of newness above the perfume of the sea—this boat was fresh. Barely used. And incredibly expensive; his throat beat a pulse of appreciation amid the nerves and the caution and the confusion. He bet it was a Sunseeker; one of the UK's most opulent ocean-going pleasure craft, built just up the coast from his Devon home, over the border in Dorset. It must be, what, forty metres long? Huge. He'd seen one at a boat show a few years back—smaller than this—and had made a mental note that one day he would own one. His father's yacht was pretty impressive, but the Sunseeker . . . it gleamed of wealth and status. And here he was. Aboard the boat of his dreams—but very likely in some kind of nightmare. Wasn't that always the way? He was a Cola after all. Things always turned nightmarish sooner or later.

He reached the sky deck.

There were five people on it. Three men and two women. They didn't notice him for a few seconds as he stood, gripping the top of the stairwell railing. One man, in white chef's fatigues, was attending to the barbecue, flipping thick steaks and adjusting a line of pepper and mushroom kebabs. Next to him a plump, middle-aged woman in a white blouse and black skirt was opening a bottle of what looked like champagne. They both looked Mediterranean, with dark hair and olive skin. A short distance away from the staff, a tall lean man with blond hair and a deep tan lay stretched out on a white leather sun lounger, wearing only shorts. He was engrossed in lively conversation with another older man who had dark grey hair and was perched on the edge of a neighbouring lounger, wearing what appeared to be a captain's uniform, minus the hat. Between these two, apparently oblivious to the conversation, reclined a girl in a lime-green bikini. Her long dark hair rippled past her shoulders and was occasionally played with by the gentle sea breeze. She had mirror sunglasses on, disguising her eyes, but her skin was golden and flawless and her full mouth was painted with red lipstick.

And she must have had her eyes open behind the shades, because she was the first one to sit up, prodding the lean, blond-haired man as she did so, and nodding towards the new arrival. The man sat up too, twisting towards him, and a smile—which seemed oddly familiar—broke out across his face.

'Hello, Spook,' he said. 'I'm so pleased you've joined us.'

Spook stared at him, astounded by his easy manner. He behaved as if this was the most normal meeting in the world. As if welcoming a complete stranger to lunch on a multi-million pound motor yacht in the middle of a mystery ocean—when the last place that stranger remembered was a coach crash in Cumbria—was an everyday occurrence.

Spook stopped himself blurting out the most obvious questions. *Who are you? Where am I?* In spite of the threat of this situation he had become acutely aware of the girl, especially now that she'd removed her sunglasses and was regarding him with an appraising smile, through cat-like green eyes. He wanted to be cool.

He tilted his head to one side, narrowing his eyes at the man, who was now on his feet and walking over the deck towards him, smiling even more broadly.

'You must be hungry,' he said, patting Spook's shoulder warmly.

'I am,' said Spook. He was pleased that his words came out steadily. His insides were vaulting about.

'Come—sit down,' said the man. 'Let me introduce you to everyone.' He led Spook to his own lounger, next to the girl, moving himself sideways onto another. Spook sat and glanced around, raising an eyebrow in what he thought was a James Bond-ish fashion. *Keep it up,* he told himself. *Illusion is all.* He wasn't about to try any genuine—Cola—illusion in front of these people. He'd been well trained to instinctively keep his secret. But he was well aware of the value of even the most everyday front. Mask yourself. Always. That was his mantra.

'This is Captain Devlin,' said his host, and the man in the uniform smiled thinly and held out his hand. Spook took it wordlessly and shook back, his eyebrow still arched. 'Over here, preparing our lunch, are Amalia,' he nodded towards the white-bloused woman who nodded back, keeping her eyes down and smiling deferentially, 'and Crisanto.' The man looked up and smiled at Spook, giving a stiff bow, before turning his attention back to the gleaming stainless steel barbecue. 'And to your right,' went on the man, 'is Kamilah, my assistant.'

31

Spook turned to take the hand that Kamilah held out to him. Her fingers were long and slender with polished almond-shaped nails—and warm when they touched his. She smiled and looked intently into his eyes, pushing back a stray lock of hair that fell across her cheek. She was breathtakingly beautiful. Probably around eighteen or nineteen. Spook's eyebrow sank back to its normal position, unheeded, and his mouth dropped open just a little. She noticed and her smile deepened. 'I am *very* pleased to meet you properly, at last,' she said, in a low, sweet voice—her accent was very slightly different to the Americanized English tones of her companions. It hinted at Eastern European but Spook couldn't be sure.

'Pleased to meet you too,' he said, and there was an unwelcome croak in his voice.

'And my name is Max,' went on his host and Spook turned to look at him and shake the hand, his guard lifting again. For a second time, as he looked into the man's face, he felt that sense of familiarity. He narrowed his eyes again, trying to chase the tiny signals in his subconscious. Where had he seen this man before? He was in his late thirties or early forties and there was something *so* familiar . . .

Max waited, gazing back at his guest with an amused smile, as if waiting for Spook to work it out. Eventually he said, 'Well . . . do you know me, Spook?'

Spook stared back, running his fingers absently through his hair and trying to remain calm. Maybe he had been concussed. Maybe he had amnesia . . . yet he felt certain that, even if the face *did* seem so familiar, he had never met this man—or anyone else here—before.

'Let me help you out,' said the man, at last. 'I'm better known as—'

'Max,' cut in Spook as the realization suddenly arrived in his mind with a flurry of additional information. TV shows, newspaper cuttings, Magic Circle features. Max Carlyle was what Spook one day hoped to be. A celebrity magician.

The man grinned and nodded.

'Max,' repeated Spook, shaking his head. 'Max Carlyle.' He began to wonder again whether he was still unconscious—in a coma perhaps. But if so—why choose *this* man to star in his personal mind movie? Max Carlyle was quite successful— but nowhere near the level of David Blaine or Copperfield or Derren Brown. Max Carlyle? His subconscious really should be aiming higher. He closed his eyes for a moment and then could hold back the questions no longer. 'Why . . . what . . . what the hell is going on?'

Max slapped him on the shoulder and let out a laugh. 'You might well ask! What the hell *is* going on? Last thing you remember is the coach, right? The crash?'

'Yes,' said Spook. He felt hostility rise up in him. The coach crash (*Darren?*) was no laughing matter as far as he could see.

'Relax,' said Max, swiftly registering his guest's expression and becoming more serious. 'You're OK. And everyone else is OK too. Nobody was killed.'

'And you know this . . . how?' Spook's hostility wavered . . . and held. He was a Cola. A *Cola*. He was important. One of Britain's most valuable assets. And he was clearly no longer in Britain. And there were clearly no Cola project people here. Wherever—*whatever*—this was, it was not sanctioned by his government. Did these . . . pampered sunbathers . . . even *know* what they had?

'Spook, I appreciate you must feel disoriented,' said Max. 'You've been asleep—recovering— for two days. We got you out of the crash and we brought you here for your own safety. You were never in serious danger—we saw to that.'

Spook caught his breath and glanced around at the other people on the deck. The captain was sitting still, watching the exchange intently, ready to move fast if need be. He was well built for a motor yacht skipper—well trained, too, in more than just driving pleasure cruisers. It was obvious. If you regularly spent time with elite soldiers, as all Colas did, you soon learnt to recognize them. Kamilah was leaning back on her lounger again, sliding one well-shaped foot across her knee. She had put her sunglasses back on but was still watching the exchange with fascination.

'You—you planned the crash,' Spook said, at last.

The man nodded, all trace of humour now gone from his features. 'Yes. We did. I'm sorry it was so brutal. It was the only way I could possibly get to meet you.'

'And why . . . ' said Spook, his heart rate speeding again, ' . . .would you want to meet me?'

'Because, Spook,' the man leaned forward, locking his eyes onto him, 'I'm your dad.'

3

It was so ridiculous he just laughed. Despite the tension and confusion, he just threw back his head and laughed.

'OK,' he said, after he'd caught his breath. 'If you say so. And . . . er . . . what shall I tell my *other* dad? You know . . . my *actual* dad.'

'Don't tell him anything,' smiled Max. 'He's not important.'

Spook felt the temporary cover of humour begin to slide off him again. A chilly draught of sea air slid through a gap in the glass windbreaks and planted a cold spot on the back of his neck. Or maybe that was just fear nudging at him again. He felt impatient. If he was in danger he wanted to know what *kind*.

'I think you should take me home,' he said,

quietly. 'Because kidnapping me was a very big mistake. You *will* regret it.'

'Spook, Spook, Spook!' Max shook his unfeasibly blond head and his well practised smile returned and deepened. 'Don't you see *anything* in me at all? Don't you have some sense of recognition?'

'Of course I do,' snapped Spook. 'You're a magician. A quite good one. Nothing earth shattering. I think you made a small impression at the FISM event in Blackpool a couple of years back . . . sold a few Max Carlyle magic sets for under tens at Davenports . . . got some minor telly work.' Spook subscribed to *Genii* and *MagicSeen* and nearly every other magician and illusionist publication going and read every page voraciously. Like all Colas he was denied internet access at Fenton Lodge, so the printed material or DVDs had to do. And he remembered it thoroughly because, like all good showmen, he had been practising memory tricks for years.

Max grinned. 'Did you see me on the Channel 4 series?' he asked.

'The reality show?' Spook curled his lip. 'When you impressed that air-head glamour model with two rubber bands? I was knocked out. No, really… on the floor.' His eyebrow was up again.

'You watched it,' pointed out Max.

Spook shrugged. 'Your party tricks didn't stick in my mind. It was more to do with her choice of swimwear.'

'But you *did* watch,' went on Max. 'Of course you did. What else would you watch?'

Spook felt his shoulders set like granite. This man—this preposterous man—who claimed to be his father, had clearly done some homework.

'You should try to understand, I have a collection service,' explained Spook. 'All the latest magician or illusionist stuff out there; I get a regular updates, in print or on DVD. I see *every* magic act. You're nothing special. And you're not my dad. Now—' He stood up and stared the man down. 'Isn't it time you got your captain to power up the engines and start motoring back to land? You can drop me at the nearest British Consulate, and if I get there unharmed I might not tell them which way you went.'

Spook felt he was doing a good job of out-bulling Max Carlyle. Yet he couldn't deny that he was fascinated. He badly wanted to know why he was sharing a luxury motor cruiser with a celebrity magician. And he guessed he was going to find out sooner or later, because there was little chance his posturing would change the man's plan—not if he was capable of turning over an armoured coach and plucking him out past a crew of Special Ops bodyguards. Of course, he himself had something more than glitter up his own sleeve and he might very well have to use it if necessary. It would need some thought though—an illusion that he could make use of to get himself home. Cheesy shock tactics and party pieces weren't going to be enough.

He was distracted from this flurry of calculations by a touch on his shoulder. He turned to see the girl—Kamilah—running her fingers down his arm. She was fixing him with her sultry green stare. 'Don't be angry, Spook,' she said, wrapping her hands around his arm. 'Please, don't be angry. You will like us. I promise you. You'll be glad you came. Very glad.'

Spook gulped. 'I didn't come. I was brought. Unconscious. Didn't really have much choice.'

'No,' she said, touching his cheek. 'From what I've heard, you don't get much choice at any time in your life.'

He gulped again. 'And what have you heard, exactly?'

'Spook,' said Max, 'we know all about the Children Of Limitless Ability. We know you are one. One of the most powerful. One of the True Eleven.'

The words shocked Spook silent. Until this point he hadn't actually believed that the outside world truly knew anything. Even though last year he and ten others had been abducted and came close to being sold off in a global auction, he had still not really accepted that the world knew about Colas. It seemed too fantastical even to him—how could the normal, everyday world of reality TV and council tax and junk food and mortgages even *begin* to grasp that such a thing as a Cola truly existed?

'I know about you,' said Max, with a gentle note in his voice. 'We all do. Everyone on this boat. I can't explain how just yet—we'll come to that in time—but for now you must believe me when I say we did *not* kidnap you. We *rescued* you. From now on, Spook Williams, you're going to start to have a little more say in your own life. From this point onwards, you are no longer a slave to the British government.'

Spook felt himself sway a little, despite the warm grasp of Kamilah, who was still hanging on to him.

'He's faint,' he heard her say. 'Quick—sit him down. I think he needs to eat.'

He was seated again and soon a plate piled with spicy sliced steak fajitas was in his lap and he was wolfing them down. A cold glass of lemonade was in his hand and he paused long enough to swallow it back in one long-held breath. He finished the food and felt enormously improved. The gnawing fear inside him seemed to have let up. Wherever he was and whatever was happening, nobody seemed to want to assassinate him. In fact, they seemed to be doing all they could to charm him. They must want something from him. Cola power.

At last, sated and calm, he turned back to Max, although it was tempting just to keep watching Kamilah, who was sitting close by on his right and apparently raptly interested in his every move. 'Tell me then, Max,' said Spook. 'What makes you think you're my dad?'

'Before I answer that,' said Max, 'what makes you certain that the man back in Devon who *says* he's your dad, actually is?'

'Well, I dunno,' shrugged Spook. 'Birth certificate,

a lot of very nice birthday presents, the only man putting his hand up to it for the last sixteen years, maybe? My mum being married to him . . . these seem like fairly good clues.'

'Do you love your father?' asked Max.

The sea breeze picked up the hair on his crown again and stirred it as if his real father was here, ruffling his hair in a matey way to encourage the correct answer. Except his father never did ruffle his hair in a matey way—and hadn't done so for as long as he could remember. He ruffled Oliver's hair. Oliver was nearly twelve now, but still very ruffle-able. And Emma, at nine, still got full-on hugs. Spook, half-brother to them both, qualified for a swift pat on the shoulder once in a while. And that was more like a repulse than a sign of affection.

'Maybe he doesn't . . . connect with you.' Max's voice slipped into his thoughts; soft; understanding. 'It can't be easy—him all that way down south. And when you do meet, you're never really alone, are you?'

It would make no difference, Spook reflected. Even if he and Gordon Williams had been locked in the same room for a month, with no communication from the outside world (let alone the ever present government surveillance they tolerated at Fenton Lodge), he doubted he would qualify for a head ruffle in that time.

'Have you ever wondered why you and Gordon have never connected?' asked Max. The smile had gone now and he seemed serious . . . genuine.

'It's not easy losing your wife . . .' said Spook. 'And being left with one weird son as a consolation prize.'

'Harder still when it's not even your own child,' said Max.

Spook snapped out of his reverie. 'Who the hell are you? What gives you the right to start poking around in my private life? You don't know him. You don't know me. You didn't know my mother! What cheap kind of trick are you trying to pull?'

Max nodded to the captain, who had remained in place throughout the meal and this new burst of discussion. He reached across to a polished dark-wood table which stood low beside his seat and pulled out a drawer. From the drawer he took a leather-bound folio and handed it across to Max. Max opened it and slid out a picture. 'I did know your mother, Spook. Very well. See for yourself.'

And he passed a picture across. It was a colour

photo. Max was in it, with a thicker head of hair and less of a tan, wearing a ruffled white shirt and a black and silver waistcoat—dressed for an early magic gig, Spook guessed. Max's left arm lay around the shoulders of a woman. A woman Spook instantly recognized, with a thud deep in his chest. Her long red hair fell in a tumble of ringlets, well past her shoulders. She was laughing at whoever was taking the photo, her beautiful dark amber eyes dancing with fun. And her arm was tightly around the waist of Max Carlyle.

Spook felt sick.

'Louisa was with me first, Spook,' said Max. He looked sad. 'We were together for nearly a year before she left me for Gordon Williams. Guess she thought he was a better bet as a father for you.'

Spook narrowed his eyes at Max, willing himself not to believe it. This sense of recognition was purely about seeing him on TV. That was all.

'She probably made the right call,' said Max, with a sigh and a rueful purse of his lips. 'I was a struggling young performer—still hadn't got my act together. Although I wasn't bad. I was attracting attention by then. Did some shows around the festivals which saw me on the up. I like to think she really loved me . . . but had to make a tough decision. I wasn't in a position to look after a family.' He sighed again and there was a wet glitter in his eyes when he looked up again. 'It must have been . . . so hard. *So* hard when she died.'

He had played it beautifully, right up to that point, Spook thought, as a sour twist knotted his full belly. The tears were what Max Carlyle probably saw as his masterstroke, but Spook had seen them before. On that dismal reality TV show Max had been in. What was it? *Celebrity Cabin Fever*? Ten people—low rent actors, ageing models, witless socialites and failed pop singers along with a fame-hungry magician— marooned in a log cabin in the Scottish highlands and made to do stupid pranks and dares to get fed. A bunch of furless animals performing in a zoo. And of course, each of them had a carefully staged 'breakdown' at least twice. Max's 'breakdown' involved the gnawed lower lip, the tremble in his jaw, the slightly wet eyes peering into the middle distance. It was the point at which Spook, watching on the small DVD player screen while he sat cross-legged on his bed, endlessly working on perfecting his card shuffling, had rejected Max Carlyle as any kind of role model. The point at which he had flipped open the machine and chucked the disc into the bin, in fact.

All of this passed through his mind as Max drivelled on about how losing Louisa was the greatest blow in his life. 'And you have to believe, Spook . . . I didn't *know*. I had no idea she was pregnant. I didn't know you even existed until a few months ago.'

'And how did you find out?' asked Spook, eyeing the distant horizon as if he too were awash with memory and emotion. He wasn't. He was focusing. Hard.

'Well, let's just say that a friend enlightened me. And . . . I have to tell you, it's been a tough time. Trying to come to terms with it all . . . with poor Louisa dying so young. So tragic . . . '

Spook's focus wavered for a second as he fought vainly to hold off the image of his mother lying dead on the kitchen floor, her eyes glassy and opaque like those of fish in a supermarket; a lock of hair across her chin. How could he really remember that, anyway, when he'd only been three?

'And then to learn *you* existed . . . for years and years . . . and I never knew. Never had the chance to be a dad to you. Never held you. And then the news that you were so special, but trapped in some boarding school . . . controlled . . . watched . . . microchipped.' Max underlined the depth of his emotion with another jaw tremble and Spook's focus returned.

There was a launch under the hull. He knew this because he'd seen this model of Sunseeker before. It had its own launch. And life rafts. But he would choose the launch. He watched the horizon again.

'I can't believe what Gordon Williams has let them do to you,' went on Max, reaching for Spook's arm. 'I can't believe . . . ' there was an artful break in his voice, ' . . . that my boy . . . '

But what Max couldn't believe *next* was never to be discovered because this was the point when Kamilah started screaming. She leapt to her feet and stared out to sea, her lovely face contorted with horror. Behind her the catering staff paled and clutched at the nearest support, the woman crossing herself, Catholic-style.

Spook stood up and followed their gaze, just as Max and Devlin did, and there was an aghast shout from the captain as he ran for the bridge. Max grasped the handrail and got down to some seriously offensive language.

Rolling towards them on the horizon, scattering terrified seabirds before it, loomed a twenty metre wall of water. As they watched, what looked like a small grey Navy frigate was thrown, spinning, through it. The tidal wave bore down on them at horrifying speed and everybody knew it was pointless to attempt any escape. As the cook sobbed out prayers and Kamilah screamed helplessly, the urgent Maydays of Devlin on the bridge could just about be made out above the rumbling approach of certain death. Max Carlyle clung to the steel rail, his face ashen beneath the tan, too petrified to even look at his newly found 'son'.

The exquisite super-sleek motor yacht—and all the people aboard it—were doomed.

4

Spook ran down the narrow walkway to the stern of the vessel and found what he was looking for. A tight metal stairwell down to the very bottom deck. And there, docked neatly, just as he expected, was a small motorboat. Two water scooters were also lodged beside it, held up clear of the water in metal grasps. Spook's blood was surging through his veins and roaring in his ears. He knew he didn't have much time. He had held the sight-line out to sea for as long as possible as he'd pelted down the stairs but now he was no longer looking, everything could go wrong at any minute.

Remote illusions were hard. Very hard. And even though he was the best Cola illusionist in existence, even he couldn't remotely maintain a full blown incoming tidal wave before five sets of eyes for more than thirty seconds. It was going to fade at any moment if he didn't get this boat out and get his sight-line back again.

For the first time in his life, Spook blessed his father's inflexible approach to sail training. As soon as he was old enough to walk, Spook had been taken sailing with his father. The experience was indelibly etched in his mind. Rather than idyllic sun-washed memories of father–son messing about on the water, it was as if he'd been recruited straight from nursery into the Royal Navy. Gordon Williams had drilled, hectored, and barked endlessly until his son jumped to every command as if he'd been electrocuted. By the time he was six, Spook was a very able sailor with his own Mirror dinghy and as handy as any experienced crew on a large yacht, although only as useful as his infant school strength could allow. Handling an outboard motor was easier than riding a bike.

So Spook detached the vessel from its mooring, gunned the motor and was out on the clear smooth sea within ten seconds. The tidal wave was just beginning to fade when he locked his eyes onto it and gave it another boost, throwing in a small red ferry, ripped open, with a scattering of drowning passengers, for good measure.

Of course, had it been real, the wave would have obliterated the motor cruiser by now . . . and surely it wouldn't be long before Captain Devlin worked that out. Spook needed to create a secondary illusion to mask his escape for the moment when Max and the captain realized they'd been duped and began to search for him. He could still hear shouts and screams, though, so for now . . . Spook allowed himself a smirk as he sped out across the aquamarine waves. He felt a little guilty about freaking out Kamilah. She seemed to be an innocent party in this . . . whatever 'this' had been. But recalling how his power had brought about such an almighty effect on her was also exciting, he couldn't deny it.

After another twenty seconds Spook stopped bothering with his frequent over-the-shoulder glances to maintain the tidal wave and let it fade. He turned the motorboat south, fleeing at an angle to the Sunseeker, so he could keep it in the corner of his eye and maintain a broadside illusion around his own vessel, just big enough to mask himself, the boat, and the wake it was churning up. He focused on water. Smooth, aquamarine water, just like all the water around him. It was a very easy illusion. Masking himself with illusion in a town or a city was much harder, as he had to focus intently on every surface he passed, so he could throw out the illusion of the view his physical presence would be blocking. It was not the same as being an invisibility glamourist like Barry, back at the lodge. Barry could simply vanish without any effort. For an illusion glamourist, though, rolling perfect camouflage was exhausting. It was much easier merely to throw a distraction illusion of being someone else, if he didn't want to be spotted. *That* he could carry easily in his head and project all around him without breaking a sweat . . . but it wouldn't work here. The sea though, was easy—easier even, as the illusion he needed to throw was here all around him to be copied and projected.

As Spook's heartbeat eased down from red alert to amber he began to think. More clearly. And he realized he'd been . . . hasty. No. He might as well admit it. He'd been stupid. For one thing, where the hell was he going? He had *no idea* where he was or in which direction he should travel to reach land. He could see his father's expression of disappointment clearly in his head. 'Only a fool, Spencer, sets out to sea without a plan,' said Gordon Williams, one greying eyebrow raised in contempt. Spook had gone badly adrift one morning as he and a friend had tried to sail a Wayfarer to a remote Cornish cove from the Williams's berth in Seaton on the South Devon coast. They had left the local coast chart behind. The boys got a tow from an RNLI lifeboat eventually, after getting caught in a riptide. Then, in front of an RNLI guy and his twelve-year-old friend—a holidaying boy whom he'd only met a week before—his father had given him a caustic dressing down. He was banned from sailing for a month and made to clean the boat from top to bottom instead. His father told him he was old enough to know better. He had been eight.

'Well, you'd love this, Dad,' muttered Spook, aloud. 'I've marooned myself again. And . . .' Far away to the west now, the Sunseeker engines powered up, the sound travelling easily on the light sea breeze. '. . . it's all been completely pointless. They're tracking me on radar. And there's not one illusion I can throw from this distance which will change that.'

Five minutes later the cruiser was alongside.

'Kamilah is ill with shock,' said Max, leaning out

from the outboard dock, looking grey and grim. 'We've put her to bed. Is that what you wanted, Spook?'

Spook said nothing, but switched off the motor.

'I'm not going to force you to get on board,' went on the man who claimed to be his father. 'And if you really want to get away, you need to head north-west. That's the nearest land. Keep going south and I don't fancy your chances in the shipping lanes—or when you reach the Algerian coast.'

'This is the Mediterranean?' said Spook.

'The Mediterranean, yes,' said Max. He pointed east. 'That way for Italy.' And then north. 'That way for France.'

Spook eyed the French direction but he was hit with a wave of tiredness.

'Or,' said Max, 'we can forget all about the last half hour and you can come in, have a cup of coffee, and we can start again. It's your choice, Spook. I'm not your jailer.'

Spook knew he was beaten. If he had any clue how far away the French coast was he might try for it, but he didn't. He had no idea whether there was enough fuel in the tank or fresh water under the seat. And, in spite of himself, he was curious . . . excited even. He wanted to find out what was going on here.

Max put out his hand and Spook took it.

5

'Here. Drink this. I think we both need it,' said Max.

He handed Spook a cup of mocha coffee, hot, sweet, and frothy. Spook set it down on the low table between them. They had gone into Max's private cabin—a beautifully appointed lounge which led into a palatial bedroom and en suite beyond—even grander than the one Spook had woken up in. The dark wood and pale suede and thick cream carpets were here in the lounge too, but there was a small crystal chandelier above the table; the windows were not portholes but expanses of tinted glass, offering a panoramic view of the sea on two sides, drifting past faster now as they were motoring and heading north. A drinks cabinet, filled with glasses, decanters, and bottles, dominated one short wall, and a retractable cinema screen filled another. Max lifted a bottle in one hand and upended a shot of brandy into each of their mugs. Spook tried not to look impressed, but he experienced a small surge of pleasure. It was good to be treated as another adult. He took a sip and savoured the heady tang amid the hot mocha.

'How's your wrist?' asked Max, eyeing the cast, which was less pristine now, splashed with sea water and sweat after Spook's recent adventures.

'A bit sore,' shrugged Spook. 'OK.'

'It was in quite a mess,' said Max. 'Stabbed through with a metal rod. You were lucky it missed your artery.'

'Could have been worse,' said Spook, drily. 'Could've been through my neck.'

Max sighed. 'I hope you'll forgive me one day, Spook. But you, of all people, must know that there was very little chance I would ever have got to meet you if I'd just gone up to the government Cola Project department and said please.'

Spook did know it. 'My friend,' he said. 'Darren Tyler. Is he OK? He was bleeding. Badly.'

'He's fine,' said Max. 'I was told he'd just bashed his nose quite severely but that's all.'

Spook paused, weighing the man's words. 'Who told you that? Who got me out of there?'

Max smiled. 'You'll meet him soon. We're heading into St Tropez this evening and he'll be at my show.'

'Your show?' echoed Spook. This was too surreal.

'Yes—I've a long-standing booking at Les Caves du Roy.'

Spook gave him a blank look.

'It's one of the most exclusive, expensive clubs in France,' explained Max, with a smug smile. 'Which is how they can afford me.'

'They book magic acts?' asked Spook, surprised. 'In night clubs?'

'And they pay a lot better than theatres,' said Max. 'The clientele is heavy with jaded multi-millionaires who like to be surprised and amazed. And I'm happy to oblige. They tip extraordinarily well.'

'OK,' said Spook. 'So . . . we meet this person at La Cave—'

'Les Caves,' corrected Max, '. . . du Roy. Yes, the collector will be there and he is very, very excited at meeting you again. The last time he met you, you were semi-conscious and screaming, so it was difficult to chat.'

'The collector?' Spook grinned and shook his head. 'What—capital T, capital C—*The Collector*? You're kidding?' Spook sniggered into his cocoa dusted froth. 'Sounds like a baddie from a 1980s Bond movie—or *Doctor Who*. What's his proper name?'

Max gave a tight smile. 'I don't know,' he said. 'He won't say. And Spook . . . however hilarious you think his name is, don't treat him lightly when you meet him. He's . . . very important. To both of us.'

'OK, OK.' Spook bit down on his laughter. 'Whatever you say.'

'Now . . . back to the little stunt you pulled earlier,' said Max. 'I am embarrassed to say I was completely fooled for a while there. And I've pulled off some pretty good mass deceptions myself over the years.'

Spook smirked into his drink. 'Sorry about Kamilah,' he said.

'She didn't know the detail of your powers,' said Max. 'She knew you had *some* power, as did my staff, but only the captain and I knew the nature of it. The staff are all pretty shaken up too. You might want to say sorry when you see them next.'

'I might,' said Spook.

'How easy was that for you?' asked Max, studying

59

him intently and running his fingers rather nervously through his hair.

Spook shrugged.

'No,' said Max. 'Tell me—on a scale of one to ten, how hard was that glamour, Spook?'

Spook paused, calculating, and then said, truthfully: 'It was pretty hard. About a seven, I'd say. It's hard to keep one that big rolling for long— and the audio too.'

Max caught his breath. 'Audio? So that wasn't just my imagination? There was sound too?'

'Yes,' said Spook. 'Audio comes with it—but only when the visual is established. People see what I want them to see . . . and then hear what they expect to hear. But I can't make them hear anything without setting up the image first.'

'OK . . .' said Max. 'But—go on. You were saying—seven out of ten hard . . . ?'

'Yeah—but mostly because I had to run and I couldn't keep my sight-line steady. I was out of contact for a few seconds.'

'So you need to keep watching to keep an illusion going?'

'It will roll on without me for a few seconds,' said Spook. 'But then it will lose momentum and start to fade, unless I pick up my line of sight again in time. I did that today, as soon as I got clear of the dock and out on the water.'

'Amazing,' breathed Max—and he looked amazed. In fact, Spook was delighted to see, his hands were very slightly trembling.

'So—can you create an illusion in a place where you're not present?'

'No,' said Spook. 'I need to be there—or at least somewhere near it—with a clear sight-line.'

'And does everybody see the same thing?'

'Yes,' said Spook, but he wasn't being entirely truthful. He *could* tell Max about Dax Jones . . . but he didn't want to. Where was Dax Jones in his life now, anyway? Long gone, by the looks of things.

'Animals, though,' he added. 'Animals aren't fooled.'

'Really?' Max sat up straight, looking fascinated.

'Really,' said Spook. 'The gulls you saw fleeing from the tidal wave were illusions too. A real bird wouldn't have seen it. It's tuned to the human brain only.'

Max seemed to digest this information for a long time, so Spook finished his drink, noticing that the sun was beginning to set to the west, casting long orange fingers across the undulating sea.

'You should go in and see Kamilah,' said Max, emerging from his thoughts, suddenly. 'Talk to her. Reassure her that you won't frighten her again. She may be an excellent assistant to me in my shows—but she's still very young and not at all prepared for what you can do. I need her all better for tonight.'

'Oh—she's your on-stage assistant,' said Spook, surprised. 'She's not your . . . er . . .'

'My what? Girlfriend?' Max gave a shout of laughter. 'Spook, you flatter me. I'm a little old for someone like Kamilah, don't you think? No—she's my very lovely assistant. You'll see her do her thing tonight. Go and see how she is now. She's in the next cabin along from yours.'

'OK—I'll go and see her,' said Spook, with a pleasant tightening in his belly. He'd be happy to. 'But, Max . . .'

'Call me Dad.'

'No. Max . . . I want to understand how you know about me?'

'The Collector,' said Max. 'He's the friend who told me about your existence. That was when we first met, a few months ago. He is a man of extraordinary talents himself . . . and he knows a

62

lot of secrets. Very high level secrets. He discovered your true parentage and came to find me.'

'Why would he do that?' asked Spook. 'What does *he* get out of it?'

'You're very cynical for a fifteen-year-old, Spook.' Max smiled and leant back into a corner of the Italian leather couch.

'I'll be sixteen in two weeks,' pointed out Spook. 'And I've had four years to grow cynical. Since I became a Cola I've been kidnapped, tested, microchipped in my brain, almost sold in an illegal international auction and nearly killed more times than I want to remember. It gives you trust issues. So—what does The Collector want? And what do *you* want?'

Max nodded, pursing his lips and reaching again for the brandy bottle. 'You're sharp, Spook. I like that in you. What do I want? I want my son. I want to show you the life you've never had . . . and together, oh boy . . . together we can have *it all*. With my talents and showmanship and experience . . . and your . . . gift. Imagine it! We will dominate the magic world. We'll be untouchable.'

Spook felt his insides clench with excitement.

This man—whether he was his blood father or not—spoke his language. Being a world-famous illusionist was his deepest desire, his biggest ambition. Not only because of all the glory—and he was certainly in it for glory—but because it offered him his one hope of freedom. If he could hide his Cola power in plain sight by pretending it was all brilliant trickery, he could have something approaching a *life*.

'OK—so that's you. And I'll buy that for now.' He nodded. 'But this Collector guy—like I said—what's in it for him?'

'You can ask him yourself,' said Max. 'We meet him in St Tropez tonight.'

Spook knocked on Kamilah's door, half expecting her not to answer. Maybe she was angry with him . . . or afraid of him. He wasn't sure which he preferred. After a few seconds she called him in, so he opened the door and stepped into her cabin. It was very similar to his own, but slightly smaller, with many more feminine touches, such as the trinkets and cosmetics on a dressing table and a wardrobe, its sliding door half open, revealing a rail of shining or glittering outfits and a tangled spill of high-heeled shoes.

Kamilah was lying on her bed, a lilac cashmere throw across her hips and legs, wearing a white silk camisole top. She leant up on one elbow, brushing her long dark hair off her face and over her shoulder. 'So, Spook Williams,' she said, in a low voice, her green eyes regarding him cautiously. 'Have you come to frighten me again?'

Spook felt a little hot. He did his best to look cool. He perched on the corner of the bed and smiled solicitously. 'I'm sorry, Kamilah. I didn't mean to scare you.'

'Oh but you did,' she said, sitting up and leaning towards him, a smile just touching her mouth. 'You definitely did.'

'Well—OK—I did,' admitted Spook, with a short laugh. 'But only because I wanted to get away.'

'Why?' She took his left hand, running her fingers along his palm and then up onto the cast. 'Don't you want to stay with us? Isn't this a beautiful place to be?'

'Ye-es,' agreed Spook. 'But it would have been nice to be *asked* rather than ambushed. I find kidnapping puts a guest in a funny mood, don't you?'

She giggled and suddenly seemed younger than the eighteen or nineteen he had first taken her for. 'You are funny,' she said, still holding his fingers but now lifting her other hand to his cheek and stroking it gently. 'You know Max will let you go if you really want to leave. He is a good man. He just hopes . . . we all do . . . that you will want to stay.'

Spook swallowed and a click sounded in his throat. He had never sat this close to such a beautiful girl before. He really didn't want her to notice how flustered it made him. 'Well,' he said, staring out of the porthole window in an effort to collect himself, 'I haven't decided yet, whether I'll stay. I have agreed to go into St Tropez with Max, though. I'd like to see his show.'

'My show too,' said Kamilah, hugging her knees and looking as excited as a six-year-old at a birthday party. 'You'll see me too, Spook.'

'Yes . . . that will . . . definitely be worth seeing,' said Spook. He took a steadying breath. 'And of course I want to meet . . .' his lips puckered with amusement, '. . . The Collector.'

The girlishness left Kamilah's face rapidly. 'Yes,' she said. 'You must meet him.'

'Who is he? What do you know about him?' Spook looked back at her, more collected now that she'd let go of him and stopped the flirting. Not that he had exactly minded that.

She shrugged. 'I've never met him,' she said. 'But I know he's . . . very powerful. Our lives changed after Max met him. A lot. All this . . .' She waved at the opulence around them. '. . . came *after* The Collector arrived.'

'For the better?' asked Spook, raising an eyebrow.

She stretched back on her satin pillows, extending her long golden-tanned arms elegantly, like a ballet dancer, and allowed a sleepy, contented smile to drift across her face. 'Definitely for the better,' she purred, and licked her lips. 'You'll see, Spook. From now on, *everything* gets better.'

Spook got to his feet. 'I've got to go and get changed,' he said, hoping the flush he could feel racing up his throat didn't reach his face before he left the room. 'I'll see you when we berth.'

'You will,' she promised.

The cold sea air hit his face and he gasped as the cabin door closed behind him. Kamilah was dizzying. And she clearly liked him. A lot.

For the first time since waking up on this boat,

Spook allowed himself to really smile. Whatever was going on here, it wasn't bad. It wasn't bad *at all*.

6

He could hardly take his eyes off his jacket. It was exquisitely designed soft black leather with a purple silk lining and a sleek retro cut which seemed to meld into his body, moving fluidly with him as he walked along. Armani, he noted, with immense satisfaction. Underneath it he was wearing a clinging dark blue sweatshirt, which made him very glad he'd kept up his swimming sessions and maintained a firmly muscled belly, and black chinos which—again—fitted him to perfection. He'd looked for leather or suede boots in the Aladdin's cave of a wardrobe he had discovered, but found none, so stuck with the deck shoes and no socks look. And as he and Captain Devlin wandered up the avenue towards the club he was glad of it. It was definitely the look of the summer—virtually

69

every other young man he saw was in deck shoes or espadrilles. If the leather jacket hadn't been so incredibly light and fine, it would have been too much on this warm evening.

The road was busy with tourists and the early party crowd. It didn't seem that early to Spook—it was nearly 11p.m.—but this, said Devlin, was early by St Tropez standards on a Saturday night. Spook was glad he'd given in to Max's insistence that he get some sleep earlier that evening. After his meeting with Kamilah, Max had come to his cabin and explained that the show wasn't on until after 11p.m., and he would need more sleep to get over the shocks of the past three days if he was to make it through to the small hours and be in a decent state to meet The Collector.

Spook had surprised himself by how readily he'd succumbed to sleep, only minutes after he drew the satin coverlet over him and sank into the pillows. He was awoken three hours later by Crisanto delivering a pre-jaunt supper, just as the twinkling lights of St Tropez came into view. As Spook wolfed down a spiced chicken casserole with exquisitely airy dumplings which Mrs Polgammon, back at the kitchens of Fenton Lodge, would have killed to get the recipe for, the boat glided into berth in one of the Riviera's most expensive marinas next to a huge red catamaran. The super-yachts and luxury cruisers around them were straight out of the movies but then, Spook had smiled to himself, so was the boat *he* was on.

Crisanto had indicated that suitable clothes were in his wardrobe . . . and he'd found some expensive hair wax, shaving gear and aftershave in the bathroom, all of which he put to good use after a slightly difficult shower in the glass tube, where his wrist cast had to be protected by a shower cap.

And now he was strolling through the warm night in one of the world's most beautiful towns, surrounded by beautiful people, dressed in beautiful designer clothes, en route to the most exclusive nightclub in France. *Just wait until you hear about this, Darren!* he thought to himself, and then felt his smile flicker when he wondered exactly *when* Darren might get to hear of this. Of course, knowing his luck, the Cola Project crack team of special operatives would swoop in any second now, and snatch him back to 'safety' before he got to taste any more of this lifestyle. Back to lessons and rules and constant surveillance and annoying kids he could do without, many of whom pretended to be underwhelmed by his powers, even after they'd gone white or choked on their tea. Colas like Dax Jones—so superior and self-important because he was the only Shapeshifter. Spook wished Jones could see him *now*. He bet that any amount of turning into a fox or a falcon wouldn't impress the beautiful people in *this* town. Foxes were vermin . . . and the French liked to shoot birds, didn't they? No, for as long as he was out of Cola Club, he was planning to enjoy himself and he wasn't going to miss any of them. Except . . . maybe, Mia. A vision of Mia's face, sweet and serene, with violet blue eyes that seemed to see right into his soul—or what shabby excuse for a soul he could claim to have—rose in his mind. He shook his head, impatiently. He didn't need *any* Cola company. He was going to be seeing Kamilah, wasn't he? And no girl he'd ever met was as gorgeous as Kamilah. His belly tightened again with excitement. He didn't expect to be impressed much by Max, but Kamilah in a sparkly magical assistant's get up . . . now that he *was* looking forward to.

'Feeling OK?' asked Devlin. He looked like an indulgent uncle, but this didn't fool Spook for a moment. He was well aware that Devlin was armed under his light linen jacket, and watching his charge very intently.

'You can relax, Devlin,' said Spook, affecting his 'medieval baron' tone. 'I have no plans to make a run for it. I'm far too intrigued about The Collector to trouble you with an escape this evening.'

Devlin smirked. 'Glad to hear it,' he said. 'I'll allow you the tidal wave—but you won't fool me so easily again. And unlike your father, I'll be less inclined to sweet-talk you round next time.'

'He's not my father,' said Spook. 'And as far as fooling you goes . . . well, we'll have to wait and see, won't we?'

Devlin cursed and brushed a white splash of gull droppings off his lapel, glancing up at the departing bird with a low curse. Spook grinned, pacing ahead of the man. There *was* no gull. There were no gull droppings, either. Oh yes. *He* was scared.

The club surprised him. It looked like a fairly ordinary hotel with the standard Mediterranean pale pink plaster on its walls and a widely arched courtyard entrance, through which a ridiculous amount of people were queuing. Devlin guided him past the line of very shiny, sparkly party people and straight to the doorman. He whispered something to him and the doorman nodded and waved them through. Spook heard the frustrated noises of the ordinary people waiting behind him, and loved it. He turned and smiled, arching an eyebrow at the slinky blonde girl closest to the front. She smiled back, lowering her chin and giving him the full benefit of her bee-stung pout and her glitter-laden false lashes. She had to be twenty-five. Oh, Spook liked this. He liked this *very* much.

Inside the club was also a surprise . . . it was very glitzy—gaudy even—with pink and gold lighting and many exquisitely good-looking women undulating on the dance floor with suntanned men who all seemed to be wearing Rolex or Breitling watches. The bar was three deep in people anxious to spend hundreds, if not thousands of euros on champagne. Devlin had told him that this was the drink of choice in Les Caves—and he had better go easy on it. That he was to get any *at all* was intensely exciting. Nobody ever got alcohol of any kind at Fenton Lodge. They were all treated like ten year olds.

Around the dance floor, which was pulsating with European pop, were many small round tables, at which some people sat (mainly men) and upon which some danced (mainly women). Devlin led him to an empty table with four chairs around it and signalled to a girl in a tight black dress. She arrived next to them as soon as they'd sat down.

'Cristal, *s'il vous plaît*,' said Devlin, and she smiled and vanished into the crowd by the bar, before returning seconds later with a bottle of champagne in a bucket of ice and two flute glasses.

'Remember,' said Devlin. 'One glass. I'm not having you puking your teenage guts all over me . . . or our guest.'

Spook glared at him but accepted the glass and drank a third of it in one hit. It took his breath away. He'd had sparkling wine before, of course— small sips at Christmas back at home, since he turned ten, even the occasional quarter of a glass at celebrations as he'd got older. But he'd never necked it like lemonade before. He struggled not to cough and snort after some of the bubbles went up his nose. Devlin smiled at him in a patronizing way. Jumped up sea-going *serf*, thought Spook. He was looking forward to throwing a seriously good illusion for this one sometime soon—not just a sneak job, like the pooing gull—for his own satisfaction. Something to make the man wet himself in terror. Spook never tired of what Darren sometimes called his 'bladder busters'. His Cola power might not have physical presence in the way that, say, Gideon Reader's did. He couldn't affect the physical world like a telekinetic could. But he could still *have* an immense impact on the people who were treated to his illusions. He could control and manipulate . . . especially non Colas, like these fools who surrounded him. It was exciting.

Part of the dance floor, near the DJ's decks, had been curtained off with black sequinned drapery and Spook guessed this was where the magic show would take place. He glanced around for the multimillionaires that Max planned to impress. There were many mature men in expensive clothes; bejewelled rings and gold watches glinting in the disco light, trophy girlfriends dancing attendance. He couldn't picture a magic show starting up in this place. It was . . . incongruous. That was the word. He felt his toes curl inside his deck shoes as he thought of it. Max was going to be embarrassing. He would have to be careful to keep a low profile—his credibility among these people

76

could be at stake if Max was his usual cheesy self and then tried to be publicly matey with him.

He took another sip of champagne, pondering on the magic act and hoping fervently that there wouldn't be a dove or a rabbit involved.

And that's when the lights went out. All of them. One second the room was a dizzying stew of pink and gold flares and glitter ball beams and the next it was completely black and the disco music cut out to nothing. A few girlish screams rose in the air but at that instant a silver orb suddenly glowed, hovering just above head height, in the middle of the dance floor, and a voice, calm and commanding, rang out through the PA system.

'Ladies and gentlemen . . . *Mesdames et messieurs* . . . Do not panic. *Ne paniquez pas.* All that you see is all that there is . . . *Tout ce que vous voyez est tout ce qu'il y a.* Please remain still and calm . . . *Veuillez rester calmes.*'

The voice went on hypnotically, switching smoothly from English to French, and back again, while the silver orb seemed to pulsate and grow bigger, drawing a few gasps from the women and begrudging grunts of surprise from the men. It drifted around in a circle, throwing a dim silver wash on the wide-eyed faces of the frozen crowd. Mysterious music arose from the sound system; a droning sub-bass with a moaning wind effect and an icy scattering of high keyboard notes, which repeated faster and faster, ramping up the excitement . . . And then the silver orb suddenly blew out streaks of light in all directions like an exploding firework and the next second everyone was dazzled by a blast of white flares and a shower of silver glitter from above. There were squeaks and shouts of excitement as a dark silhouette emerged amid the effects. The black sequinned curtains had been drawn back and there stood Max Carlyle, immaculate in a black suit and purple shirt, his hands aloft and his trademark smile in place—one brow marking a curve of 'mystery' above his eye. Applause and a few whoops ran around the room.

Spook had to admit Max had made a pretty good entrance, even though the Zombie Ball was a very well-used trick. There was nothing sophisticated about the silver orb all—just rods and black felt—mere puppetry. But it was a good visual effect to kick off with and the lighting had worked well. Now the soundtrack dropped down to an almost imperceptible bass drone and Max spoke.

'Time and space, illusion and reality . . . what does it mean to the human mind?' he asked. And then repeated it in French. The skipping between two languages was oddly mesmerizing, Spook noted, reminding himself to work harder in Mrs Sartre's French class and then shaking his head with a small shiver as he realized he might never sit in Mrs Sartre's French class again.

'What is real and what is false?' asked Max, his hair glistening with a little too much brilliantine wax. 'And where . . . on the line between these two . . . does magic lie? Perhaps, madame . . .' He stepped forward and took the hand of a beautiful blonde girl in a microscopic red dress. '. . . you can help me find out?'

The girl glanced at her partner—one of the millionaires by the look of him, thought Spook. The man, dark and Arabian looking, in his forties or fifties, gave an imperious wave, granting her to Max Carlyle. She bounced to her feet, giggling, and was led to the low stage area by the magician.

Max turned the woman, and himself, side on to the audience. 'Look into my eyes,' he said, and Spook's toes clenched in his shoes. It was *such* a cliché. What followed was a fairly predictable vanishing and reappearing card trick—but with the bonus that the nine of diamonds—the girl's choice of card (freely made as far as *she* knew)— transformed into a handful of nine *actual* diamonds falling from Max's cards. Well, *glass* diamonds, thought Spook, but the effect was the same. The audience applauded warmly as she was sent back to her wealthy man clutching the 'diamonds'. Spook was aware that most of the clapping—and a few high-pitched whoops—came from the women, who were eyeing Max with fascination.

They can't fancy him? Spook spluttered inside his mind, as appalled as he might be if Max really *was* his dad. *He's just a cheesy cruise ship conjuror!* But yes . . . they did. He glanced around the club and saw a dozen women on the edge of their seats (or tables), pouting up at Max, begging to be his next choice. Spook sniggered and shook his head and Devlin raised an eyebrow at him across his second glass of champagne. 'Suckers,' mouthed back Spook, curling his lip in contempt. He rarely used such an Americanism but it really summed up these sheep so well. They were *so* impressed by the pyrotechnics and cards and baubles and so completely unaware of how easily they were being duped. It was clever, really, to make an art form out of such basic tricks. He'd read all about them in magic magazines for the past four years and learned that there were really only eight or nine basic tricks which were constantly being reworked by new generations of showmen. He had some grudging admiration for the good ones—the slick practitioners like Copperfield or Lance Burton or Penn and Teller.

But he could not help feeling superior. What the best magicians had studied and sweated and toiled to achieve over years and years *he* possessed at the flicker of an eyelid. The only reason he was studying magic at all was to be able to fool *other* magicians. The card tricks were his first focus. Without a decent working knowledge of the Chalier or Moden cut, finger flinging and the False Shuffle he would be sunk among his peers and rivals. He had worked at these tirelessly for the last four years and was pretty good at them now. His close up coin work was very effective. The coin roll was also crucial to his credibility. Several times other Colas had just assumed he was glamouring them when he was *actually* doing it. It was important to press on with it, though, in spite of these frustrations. The sleight of hand he most needed to perfect was that he actually *had* sleight of hand. It was a peculiar and amusing little paradox. Spook loved it.

The show moved on predictably enough with more set pieces which made Spook groan inside. The Chinese Linking Rings. The Dancing Cane . . . the Vanishing Cane. Most of the audience was still rapt, taken in by the showmanship—although personally Spook felt Max was overdoing the mysterious staring into the middle distance and the elaborate 'How could *that* have happened?' shrugs. He noticed, also, as he glanced around, that the wealthy man who had allowed his girlfriend to take part in the first card trick was looking bored. Of course, men of his stature often affected an unimpressed air, but if he wasn't mistaken, Spook could see the occasional flicker of a glance from Max in the direction of this man. Perhaps this was one of the 'big tippers' whom Max was hoping to wow.

Now Kamilah arrived, in a shimmering purple dress which was little more than a see-through leotard with some strategically placed sequins and a very short fringe of beads for a skirt. Her long legs were clad in fine fishnet tights and her feet in a pair of strappy high-heeled purple sandals. A huge amethyst stone was at her throat, on a black velvet choker, and her dark hair was twisted into a high ponytail. Her eyes were made up with smoky liner and purple glitter and her lips shimmered with gloss. She looked amazing and moved like a dancer as she wheeled a trunk into the centre of the stage area and then stood tall, arms aloft, hips at a provocative angle.

Spook felt a smile weave across his face. It was worth catching Max's very average show just to see Kamilah. He managed to hang on to the smile even when he realized, with a sinking heart, that Max was going to do the Sub Trunk. *Dear God,* he thought, *it's as if he's working through the 1979 Lame Tricks Handbook. Sub Trunk has been done to death!* Maybe, though, he pondered, Max would put an interesting twist on it like he'd once seen on a Pendragons' DVD—make it fresh in some way.

Max did not add an interesting twist. The escapology routine was precisely the same as every basic version he'd ever seen. Magician ties up female assistant, bags her and puts her in the trunk. *Check.* Chains up the trunk. *Check.* Jumps on trunk and swooshes a cape about. *Check.* Drops out

of sight as she jumps up amid the swirling cape . . .
Check. Is discovered in the bag, tied up, inside the
trunk. *Check, cheesy check.*

The audience applauded and Mr Millionaire
joined in, but mainly, Spook decided, because he
was staring wolfishly at Kamilah. He still didn't look
even remotely excited about the act.

It was when Max did The Dove Cage that Spook
gave up all hope of getting impressed any time this
week. The disappearing cage, complete with a dove
inside, was so creakingly old he could have wept—
was *this* what Max Carlyle had chosen for the finale?
Even as he thought these words Kamilah danced
past him, bugle beads shaking from her hips, gave
him a devastatingly sexy smile and danced back to
the stage for the finale. Apparently the dove trick
wasn't the finale. Spook noticed a folded piece of
paper had arrived on the table beside his hand. He
picked it up and unfolded it, puzzled, and peered
at the writing in the dim light.

On stage Max was telling the audience that they
were about to be privileged to see something nobody
in the world of magic had done before. *Yeah, right,*
thought Spook as he squinted at the handwriting.
'Be ready to be astonished, amazed . . . and maybe

scared,' warned Max. 'Although I promise you . . . you are in no danger.'

Spook stared at the paper and felt blood rushing in his ears, his heart beating a fast tattoo in his chest and throat.

Whatever you like, Spook, read the note. *Now would be good.*

7

Spook froze in his seat. Max was expecting *him* to provide the final illusion? A *real* Cola illusion? His heart was now pounding so fast it almost hurt his chest and he was sucking in long slow breaths, trying to control it. Neither Max nor Kamilah so much as glanced at him. They were moving around the stage, asking for hush and concentration. The lights on the audience went to black. The lights on stage went to a steadily pulsating blue and white.

A hush fell across the room, heavy with anticipation, although off to his left Spook could see Mr Millionaire checking out his manicured fingernails.

The past four years of Cola Project training had instilled one thing into Spook Williams more than any other. NEVER show off Cola power in public.

NEVER. NEVER . . . and if you were in any doubt about when you could . . . that would be NEVER. Of course, as soon as his government had a *use* for his Cola power being shown off in public, all that would change, he had no doubt of it. And inside the walls of Fenton Lodge and around its well guarded rolling acres, plenty of breaking of the NEVER rule went on. Outside, though, Spook had only ever used his glamour in a serious emergency. And giving Max Carlyle a good ending to his sadly average magic show hardly counted as a serious emergency.

The hush was lengthening. The suspense was building . . . and in danger of just falling apart in a sea of derisive giggles. Max really had nothing? Nothing else up his sleeve? The Cola in Spook shrugged a *SO WHAT*? But the showman in Spook was in agony. Which . . . of course . . . was exactly as Max would have predicted. Spook knew he was being played. Being shoved into flexing his Cola powers on demand. Well . . . he was stronger than that.

Someone in the crowd muttered, 'Get on with it!'

Spook folded his arms and blanked Max and Kamilah.

In the corner of his eye he saw Mr Millionaire yawn elaborately.

And he broke.

Suddenly a chasm opened in the air between Max and Kamilah. A crack in time and space. Through it a wisp of cold white mist curled, writhing out towards the audience in elegant tendrils, glowing and surreal. The audience muttering ceased abruptly and Spook felt a ping of hot pleasure through his solar plexus. Everybody was staring at the chasm and the mist. Mr Millionaire had stopped yawning and sat up; his girlfriend's eyes were like saucers and she was holding her hands to her throat.

What next? pondered Spook, with more pings of hot pleasure firing through his belly. Some theme? How had Max begun the show . . . ? Waffling on about time and space . . .

An old-fashioned clock face appeared in the chasm. The chasm tore itself wider apart so the whole of the face could clearly be seen, the hands on the clock ticking jerkily around. As soon as the audience had absorbed the clock it began to tick audibly, just as their collective awareness expected. The ticking grew faster and the hands spun around the face, speeding up and up until Spook stopped them dead. He paused, looking at Max. Max glanced at him and then, with a cough, spoke.

'Time . . . space . . . illusion or reality . . .' he intoned. 'Where will it take us? Watch . . . watch and see . . .'

Spook grinned to himself. *Now* Max had them. Allowing the clock to fade he brought faces out of the mist. Faces of people in the audience. He worked quickly, glancing around and creating perfect copies of several of them, peering, wide-eyed, out of the tear in space and time, back at themselves in the real world. The girl who'd got the diamonds—pouting and giggling. One of the bar staff, balancing a tray with glasses of champagne and yawning—to much hilarity from his colleagues, spellbound behind the bar. The last one was the bored millionaire, his gold neckchain glinting in the weird illusory light and his eyes boring into the eyes of the real thing. Spook felt a warm fizz of delight as the millionaire stood up and gasped audibly.

But before the man could stride across to his doppelgänger Spook faded the image out and brought back the clock. Mr Millionaire sank back into his seat, still looking stunned. Spook began to wind the clock hands backwards, slowly at first and then faster and faster—until they were just a humming blur. What next? Hmmmm . . . How had the clientele of Les Caves looked sixty or seventy years ago? He summoned up a guess, pulled the chasm wider and showed a bar, in occupied France, teeming with stereotypical French resistance men and sultry women in berets. It was hardly historically accurate but he let it fade quickly amid the murmurs and gasps, and then took the clock back further still, turning the view through the ragged tear into a hillside forest with hunters on horseback galloping between the trees. An archer let an arrow fly and it shot straight out of the chasm towards Mr Millionaire. Spook had the greatest surge of delight as the man shouted in shock; the arrow piercing the table between his splayed fingers before vanishing in a puff of white mist. His girlfriend clutched at the air where it had been quivering a second before and squealed with amazement.

Back in the chasm, time was winding backwards again . . . further and further and further . . . And there was palpable fear in the audience now. Spook knew he had to keep a lid on it. There was thrill fear and there was abject, bowel-loosening terror fear. He could bring about both kinds, but guessed that Max was hoping the clientele would leave tonight in a haze of amazement rather than a fug of soiled underwear.

Even so . . . he would push it *just* a little further. One more little fright should do it. Inside the glowing rip in space and time the forest had faded and was now replaced by a quietly steaming primeval swamp. Everything went very still. Dragonflies skittered around the watery landscape and tiny hisses and drones wound their way through the collective consciousness. A low bass hum was building gently . . . Max seemed to sense the climax was on its way and stepped away a little; on the other side of the illusion, Kamilah did the same. Her eyes were wide and shining and her smile was fixed. Spook could see her chest rising and falling rapidly. He was scaring her. This was *so* brilliant!

The entire audience was holding its breath, eyes riveted on the illusion. Even the waiting staff and bar stewards were frozen in their work, utterly gripped. Spook counted in his head . . . *Three . . . two . . . ONE!*

A vicious hooked claw punched through the chasm, followed by the ferocious, ravening jaws of a velociraptor. Screams erupted through the audience along with a hissing bellow from the prehistoric creature. Spook was careful to keep its hind legs and tail on the far side of the chasm. If he allowed it to jump through there would definitely be a mass evacuation the like of which St Tropez's beautiful people had never seen. And not just in the 'running for the doors' sense of the word.

Spook put a zip fastener at the top end of the chasm, making it flash red a few times so Max couldn't possibly miss it. To his credit, Max got the cue immediately and, with a flourish, swept his arm up above the velociraptor's snapping jaws and made a 'grab' for the zip. Spook moved the zipper down fast, but not so fast that Max's fingers couldn't keep pace. As the zipper drew down, the cacophony of screaming, hissing, and snarling grew quieter and then, when it closed on the final notch, the entire illusion exploded in green sparks, leaving nothing above the stage but a drift of white mist.

For a few seconds there was absolute silence. And then a storm of cheering, clapping, shouting, and whooping erupted through the room. Mr Millionaire was on his feet, clapping his hands high and nodding at Max. Max took Kamilah's hand and led her into a curtsey while he took a bow. He looked absolutely triumphant, while Kamilah looked shocked rigid through her smile.

Finally Max raised his finger to his lips. Then his voice cut through the wild audience response. 'Remember the date. You have seen it here first. From Max Carlyle. Goodnight.' Then there was another dazzling blast of light and by the time everyone had blinked it away the magician and his assistant had gone.

Through the excited buzz of the astonished audience—some of whom now rushed to the stage area, waving their hands through the air and checking the curtains for signs of the fakery—Spook heard a pleasant, cultured English voice remark:

'Well, that wasn't bad for your debut, Mr Williams.'

8

The man next to him was older than Max, probably by twenty years, but his posture spoke of a much younger man. Without the white hair, from a short distance, he could have been taken for a man in his thirties, thought Spook. He sat in the chair to Spook's left, one arm resting along the back of the chair on his other side, supremely at ease. He was gazing at the scene on the stage area with an amused smile on his lips and when he turned to look at Spook, even in the dim light his eyes were a ferocious blue.

'You must be The Collector,' said Spook, and found the title less amusing now. Something about this man knocked any comedy out of it.

'And you must be Spencer Williams,' said the man, extending a hand.

'Spook—please.' He took the man's hand and found it cool and firm as he shook. He had planned, all evening, to challenge the man as soon as they met—'And what the hell gives you the right to nearly kill me and then kidnap me?'—but now that he was faced with his kidnapper the words fell out of his head. The Collector's eyes crinkled at the corners; they seemed to seek out great amusement in life.

'Spook—of course,' he said, inclining his head but maintaining eye contact. He was dressed in a black dinner suit with a white shirt, open at the collar; no tie—but he wore them as if they were jeans and T-shirt, without any ceremony at all. 'How did you enjoy your first performance in the real world?'

Spook glanced back across to the sequinned curtains and couldn't prevent a smirk. 'Well—it wasn't *my* performance, was it?'

The Collector scooped a handful of mixed nuts from a glass bowl on their table with a grin. 'It certainly wasn't Max Carlyle's,' he said. 'Or do the Zombie Ball and the Sub Trunk excite you, Spook?'

Spook snorted. 'Please,' he said.

Devlin was a seat away, watching them closely. He seemed uneasy at the arrival of The Collector, who now leaned past Spook and fixed his blue stare on the man. 'No need to babysit while I'm here, Devlin,' in a voice that was both silk and steel. 'Go and find Max and Kamilah. Tell them to join us for a drink in five minutes . . . if they can battle through their adoring public.'

Devlin seemed to hesitate for a second but then nodded and got to his feet. 'No more champagne for him,' he said, with a sidelong glance at Spook.

As Devlin stepped away The Collector poured a full glass and passed it over. Spook accepted with a grin.

'Do we need to have the conversation, Spook?' asked The Collector. He dropped two Brazil nuts into his mouth and glanced around the room as if fascinated by its inhabitants.

'The conversation?' repeated Spook. He couldn't understand why this man wasn't provoking the same hostile reaction in him that Max had. Possibly because he wasn't claiming to be his father. Or maybe just because he clearly didn't dye his hair.

The Collector swallowed his Brazil nuts, tapped his long, tapered fingers rapidly on the table top and at last brought his gaze back to Spook. 'Oh, *you know* . . . why did you abduct me? What do you want? Where will this end?'

'Well . . . now that you come to mention it,' said Spook.

'Let me be brief and to the point, so we can get past any awkwardness,' said The Collector, although Spook doubted he'd ever been awkward in his life. 'You're in no danger. Well—no—that's not the truth. You are always in danger thanks to your peculiar semi alien pedigree. I'm sure you know that already. What I mean is—you're in no more danger than you were this time last week, when you were at the tender mercy of the Cola Project. Your circumstances have been changed—that's all— and very likely for the better. If I had been able to come to see you in Fenton Lodge and outline my thoughts and plans for you, Spook, I have no doubt at all that you would willingly have signed yourself out of the Cola Project and come away with me on the spot—if such a thing were possible.' He threw back his head and laughed. 'Imagine!'

Spook stared at him, fascinated. He half believed what the man said—that was the strangest thing.

'But, of course, that could never have happened.

97

So you needed to be rescued. And I promise you, if you decide to return to your old life, I will not try to stop you—I'll even give you a lift back to Cumbria myself. Just . . . take a few days. Understand what choices you have. Can you do that for me?'

Spook nodded. He could do that. After all, how hard could it be to spend time on a luxury yacht with his every need catered for, showing off his illusions and impressing Kamilah?

'But what if they find me?' he asked. 'I mean . . . they do have a world class dowser, you know. She's probably already sent the SAS after me. Special forces could be here right now for all you know.' And it was true. Spook was expecting a rescue attempt at any time. With Lisa's amazing ability to find people around the planet, he was only surprised it hadn't happened already.

'You don't need to worry about Miss Hardman. Or Paulina Sartre . . . or any of the other Colas with dowsing talent,' said The Collector, lifting a glass and eyeing the bubbles in it with interest. 'You are protected.'

'By what?' Spook raised an eyebrow, unconvinced. There was a nerdy little non-Cola back at Fenton Lodge, called Clive, who had used all kinds of bargain bucket gadgetry to help Dax Jones and his little club avoid capture when they went on the run a couple of years back. But that had involved some cheap motion sensors, tin foil, string and hiding under chunks of granite as far as he'd been able to find out. Oh—and Mia talked about visualizing a protective mirror pyramid over your head if you didn't want to be dowsed—but that sounded even lamer.

'By me,' said The Collector. He put down the glass and took Spook's hand briefly in his. With any other person he could think of, except perhaps Mia or Kamilah, Spook would have flinched, but he did not now. There was something oddly calming about the fleeting contact, something which made his breathing slow down. How could this stranger possibly protect a Cola? He had no idea. But right now he believed The Collector could.

Max arrived at their table, jarring Spook back to reality. His eyes seemed to be backlit with excitement as he took the seat to Spook's left and clapped Spook on the back. 'I am SO proud of you, son,' he said and although he flinched a little inside, Spook didn't protest. 'That was simply astonishing. What a show! What a team!'

Max nodded at The Collector—and like Devlin, he seemed uneasy. 'I see you've met our protégé,' he grinned, not quite making eye contact.

'Indeed I have,' grinned back The Collector, tilting his head.

'A very promising start, I think,' said Max. There wasn't time for him to say much more because people kept coming up to him, marvelling at his brilliance. Men pumped his hand, shaking their heads and giving him blokey acceptance while women pouted up at him like mesmerized deer, as if hoping to be further hypnotized. Spook smirked. If just one little Cola illusion could achieve this for Max, what could it do for *him*? As if reading his thoughts, The Collector leaned over and murmured close to his ear, 'Intoxicating, isn't it? Wait until it's you…'

Now Max, with another uneasy smile and nod at The Collector, was borne away to join the table of Mr Millionaire, who had undergone a complete reversal of attitude and was now ordering more champagne for the magician and demanding his full attention. The two men fell into lively conversation and the millionaire kept prodding Max's shoulder or clapping his back, claiming a kind of ownership, it seemed.

The Collector was watching too. 'All falling into place very nicely,' he said.

'What is?' asked Spook, fascinated.

'Aaah—there is more going on here than you know, my flowering genie,' he said. 'And you'll find out all about it tomorrow—it wouldn't be wise to talk about it here. I think you'll like it. A great deal . . .' And the man rose to his feet, rested his hand on the crown of Spook's head for a few seconds and then walked away, vanishing into the crowd. Spook felt slightly dizzy and his insides fizzed with excitement. He was drinking the champagne too fast, he guessed. He should go easy—he didn't want to be swaying about and looking stupid in front of Kamilah. And here she came now, walking across the dance floor, which was now filling up again as the resident DJ returned to his decks and sent Euro pop pounding through the PA system.

Kamilah had let her hair down and it fell in soft, shining waves across her shoulders. She had changed into a short red silk dress which clung to her fabulous figure. Her feet were strapped into high-heeled black sandals. A glistening jet choker was at her throat and ruby studs glowed at her ears. She was breath-taking, turning the heads of men all around the room. And she was coming to sit with *him.*

'I don't know what to say to you,' she breathed, as she accepted the glass of champagne he'd just poured for her. Her green eyes looked dark and luminous, like a forest in twilight, thought Spook, and then felt slightly foolish at such poetic words in his head. 'I . . . I'm a little afraid of you,' she added, dropping her lashes now and toying with the champagne flute.

'You never need to be,' he said and she smiled and looked back up at him shyly. Spook had to resist punching the air. This was *off the scale* fantastic. 'They're just illusions,' he added. 'They can't hurt you. They have no substance.' Not long ago Spook would have crawled across burning coals rather than make such a statement . . . it was one of his biggest frustrations that, unlike Gideon and Luke Reader, who could make things crack apart or fly at speed with their telekinesis, *he* could not actually impact on anyone or anything in a physical way. His illusions were true mirages . . . utterly convincing but with no substance at all. And yet they could be very powerful. He'd witnessed that tonight. At Fenton Lodge the Colas were used to the assorted amazing powers that were contained within the building and its grounds and even though they couldn't help but react, at first, to the images he sometimes conjured up, they soon got blasé and shrugged them off. Even the sight of Dax Jones shapeshifting into a fox or an otter or a falcon didn't faze any of them now—and to start with, as the only shapeshifting Cola, he'd always been lapping up all the attention.

Out here in the real world, though, Spook's talent could make a roomful of wealthy partygoers scream; could make a powerful millionaire scramble to befriend a cheesy magician; could make a beautiful girl stare at him as if he was a god. Oh yeah. Bring. It. On.

9

The second day Spook woke up aboard the Sunseeker was very different to the first. Without the panic and confusion all he had to do was luxuriate in the beautiful bed in its fabulous cabin, dwelling with much smug contentment on the events of the night before.

True, he did have a headache—the result of more alcohol than his teenage constitution had ever experienced before. Although he hadn't swayed about (as far as he knew) on the way back from the club to the boat, he had been laughing a lot with Kamilah, who had wound her arm through his and leaned close to him when they'd all climbed into the hire car—a large silver Mercedes people carrier with enough space at the back for Max's magic show props.

There was a jug of water with ice and slices of lime floating in it on the low table at the end of his bed, as well as a packet of fizzing paracetamol and stomach salts, thoughtfully placed there by whoever knew how much he'd drunk last night. There was also a bowl of shortcake biscuits and ripe strawberries. Spook scrambled to the end of the bed, ripped the two tablets from their foil and deposited them in a glass with a slosh of iced water. A minute later he had quaffed the bittersweet sparkling draught and then tried a bit of shortcake and a strawberry. These went down extremely well and he began to feel better.

A flash of memory from last night fizzed his stomach up more than the salts, but this time with a thrill of deep satisfaction. He had thrown a Cola illusion. Had done it in full view of the public. He had taken a roomful of sophisticated people and bent their perception completely to his will—and in doing so had made a legend out of Max Carlyle, and a hero-worshipper out of Kamilah. Again he felt those hot pings of delight as he remembered how she had looked at him last night; the way she had clung to him and hung on his every word . . . even though he was probably making very little sense by

105

the time they'd got back to the boat—how many glasses did Max let him drink? His real father would have hit the roof!

And then she'd kissed him . . . hadn't she? Or maybe he'd dreamt that bit. Spook frowned, trying hard to remember. Outside his room, as she'd said goodnight. Yes . . . a kiss. Not on the cheek. Warm and soft. He'd stood there, grinning after her like an idiot, as she'd sashayed away to her own room, glancing back at him only once with a small, girlish wave over her shoulder.

Then he'd opened his cabin door and fallen over the high ridge step, landing face first on the thick cream carpet. He was buzzing with far too much excitement, champagne, and boosted ego to notice whether it hurt. He had never felt so utterly cool in his life. He'd fallen asleep grinning.

By the time Spook had showered his headache had all but gone and the smell of frying bacon from the top deck was calling to him. The cruiser had been sailed a little way out of port, away from all the other boats in the marina but within easy reach of St Tropez, which glowed gently in the morning sun; all terracotta pink and gold, framed by his portholes. A soft swell was caressing the bow of the boat. Spook had never been troubled with any kind of sea-sickness except once, out on a cargo ship in the middle of a North Sea storm. Here, he felt completely at ease.

Fresh clothes awaited him on the suede sofa beneath the portholes. More black jeans (whoever shopped for him seemed to know his favoured colour) and a soft merino wool jersey in mint green. He pulled them on and stepped outside barefoot, gasping at the cool morning sea breeze.

'Spook—son! Come here!' Max waved him across to the opaque blue glass breakfast table which had been set up under a wide blue sunshade on the sky deck. 'Full English? The works? You've earned it!'

Spook nodded and sat down next to Max, who appeared to be eating alone, served by Chrisanto, who was again at the open-air grill, deftly tossing mushrooms and bacon across one sizzling skillet while nursing four frying eggs on another. A basket of sliced baguette lay on the table next to a pot of butter. Spook picked up a knife and side plate and began to liberally butter a slice while Max poured him freshly squeezed orange juice.

'How's the wrist?' asked Max, with a nod towards the cast.

Spook shrugged. 'Annoying in the shower. I have to cover it up with a shower cap to stop it getting soggy. But otherwise, fine. How long will it need to stay on?'

'Only two or three more days,' said Max. 'He thinks it'll mend pretty fast.'

'Who thinks?' asked Spook. Was there a ship's doctor hidden away somewhere?

'The Collector,' said Max, through a mouthful of bacon and fried bread. He looked a little older in the fresh morning air, thought Spook. The lines on his face were highlighted by too much fake tan. Some grey roots were showing, too, through the blond dye.

'The Collector's a doctor?' said Spook. 'Is there no end to his talents?'

'He's . . . very clever,' said Max. He took a drink of orange juice and glanced around, almost nervously. 'And I owe him a lot, so please . . . less of the sarcasm. As far as I could tell, you seemed pretty impressed with him last night.'

'Well . . . he has a certain presence, I'll give you that,' said Spook, accepting a hot plate of bacon, mushrooms, fried egg, fried bread and sliced grilled tomato. 'But I still don't know anything about him. How did you two meet? Why is he involved in our lives . . . I mean—your life?'

'*Our* lives,' insisted Max. 'You'll have to accept it sooner or later, Spook. Our lives are on one path now. We'll go to a clinic and do a DNA test if that will help you believe me.'

Spook took a mouthful of egg and peered at Max with distaste. His dad? Could he really be related to a man who let his roots show? He searched for clues in the man's features. Max's nose was long and straight . . . as was his own. Max's mouth was precisely shaped . . . not *unlike* his own. Max's eyes were nothing like his, but he knew already that the eye colour and the hair colour came from his mother. That she could have been impressed enough to mate with a specimen like Max Carlyle nearly put him off his bacon.

'Why not?' he said, after a gulp of juice. 'Let's ride into St Tropez and roll up our sleeves at the nearest clinic—it'll be just like one of those daytime TV talk shows, won't it? "LAME MAGIC ACT SAYS HE'S MY DAD BUT I THINK IT'S JUST A CHEAP TRICK . . ." '

'Is that what you really think?' asked Max, looking serious and staring at his knife and fork. 'That I'm lame . . . ?'

Spook shrugged and muttered, 'Sub Trunk.'

'Have you any idea what it takes to pull off the Sub Trunk with style?' demanded Max.

'Have *you*?' asked Spook.

Max slammed down his cutlery and then took a deep breath. 'Jeeeeez,' he sighed, forcing a sickly grin across his face. 'I've heard about teenage kids. Never thought I'd have to experience it.'

'Where's Kamilah?' asked Spook, eyeing the stairwell.

'She'll be up soon enough. You kind of wore her out last night, you know. There's only so much she can take.' Max leaned back in his seat and folded his arms, a wolfish look crossing his face. 'I think you've made quite an impression there—and Kamilah's not a girl who's easily impressed.'

Spook smirked across a forkful of tomato.

'Just go easy on her, Spook,' warned Max. 'She's not as tough as she appears. I don't want her heart broken.'

Spook coughed as the tomato nearly shot into his windpipe. *Him?* Break *Kamilah's* heart?

'So,' he coughed again, 'when does The Collector come back and tell me about this master plan? He told me last night there was something bigger going on—and I'd find out what today.'

'Did he now?' Max looked interested, edgy even.

'Yes—it was all very Bond villain. Like the name,' said Spook, lightly, although he struggled to still feel the joke after meeting The Collector. He knew he'd never make gags like this to the man's face; he only wanted to wind up Max.

'All I'm really missing is the white cat, yes?' said a cool voice beside him and Spook jumped violently.

'What—? How do you *do* that?' he spluttered, wiping tomato pips off his chin.

The Collector merely smiled from the seat next to Spook. He was dressed in a dove grey linen suit and white shirt and his eyes, here in the morning light, were even more icy blue. 'There's no need to lend me Hollywood qualities just yet, Mr Williams,' he smiled. 'Flattered though I am.'

'Breakfast?' asked Max, waving Crisanto over urgently, but The Collector shook his head.

'Have you measured him yet?' he asked, casting his eyes up and down Spook's form as Spook sat back in his chair, resting his cutlery on the plate, trying not to think about his unguarded Bond villain comments.

'No. We can do it now, though,' said Max, hastily mopping his mouth with a napkin and reaching for a phone which rested in a cradle at one end of the table. He pressed a couple of numbers on it. After a pause there was a response at the other end. 'Kamilah, sweetheart,' said Max. 'Are you up and dressed yet, Sleeping Beauty? You are? Good. Can you ask Amalia for a tape measure? Yes—a tape measure. And bring it right up to the sky deck. Thank you.'

'What are you measuring?' asked Spook.

'You,' said Max.

'Erm . . . why?' asked Spook.

'Because we need to know how big you are.'

Spook pushed back his chair and stood up. 'Is this some kind of joke?'

Max and The Collector exchanged looks. The Collector smiled. 'It's very serious, Spook,' he said. 'If you measure correctly, we're all systems go.'

Spook walked to the rail and wrapped his fingers around it, taking a lungful of sea air and wrestling against the urge to shout, 'WHAT? WHAT? WHAT THE HELL IS GOING ON? WILL YOU STOP TREATING ME LIKE A SIX YEAR OLD AND JUST TELL ME?'

The Collector leaned on the rail beside him. 'I'm sorry, Spook—we're trying your patience. And I quite understand. I will explain everything very shortly, but first, here is the lovely Kamilah with a tape measure. Will you submit?'

Spook turned to see Kamilah at the top of the spiral stairwell, wearing a yellow sundress. Her hair was in a loose side plait and her face was bare of make-up. In the blue light reflecting off the sea she looked young and dewy fresh. She held up a reel of tape and let one end of it fall, spiralling, from her palm. 'Do I have permission?' she asked, teasing him with a smile.

Spook stepped towards her and held out his arms as she measured his chest, then closed them again as she measured the breadth of his shoulders and then the drop from the top of his head to the floor. She rattled off the measurements to Max as she went, and he wrote them down on a notepad. When she had finished she stood, gazing up at Spook. 'He's tall,' she said. 'Not too tall. And not too wide.'

Max seemed to be making calculations. At length he looked up and nodded at The Collector. 'It's fine,' he said. 'It'll work. Next . . . '

Kamilah handed the tape measure to Spook. 'Now,' she said, 'measure me.'

113

Spook sucked in air before he could stop himself, but he bit down quickly on his surprise and took the tape measure. 'Height—and chest and shoulder,' said Kamilah, laughing at his blush. He took the height fast with her help, holding the top of the tape on her crown. Then she put her arms at her side and nodded, 'Round—at the widest point.' Spook wound the tape around her back and pulled it past her shoulders and out to the front and then drew it close. It was some time before he could even see the numbers on the tape but eventually he gave the figure, in a voice which cracked embarrassingly.

'Thank you,' said Kamilah, stepping out of the tape measure with a prim smile and an amused green flash from her eyes.

Again Max did some calculations. 'Both have five or six centimetres to spare,' he said.

'Good,' said The Collector. 'Very good.'

'What is this all about?' asked Spook.

The Collector guided him to one of the recliner seats and sat him down. 'Spook,' he said, 'do you always do as you're told at Fenton Lodge? Are you a good boy?'

Spook snorted. 'What do *you* think?' he asked. In

truth he was hardly the school rebel, but he liked things his own way and didn't trouble himself too much about bending rules to achieve his own ends.

'I think I may be about to test you,' said The Collector, watching him closely. 'I wonder how far you are willing to bend rules?' He was dropping his voice, leaving Max and Kamilah out of the circle for now.

Spook stared at him. 'That would depend—what rules?'

'I think where you and I are concerned, few of society's rules really apply,' said The Collector, still speaking softly—one to one.

'*You* and *I*?' repeated Spook.

The Collector nodded. 'I believe you know we're both a little different from the common man,' he said. 'And so we live by different rules.'

Spook frowned and felt goosepimples break out across his arms. Any other normal man would have done nothing to dent his sense of Cola superiority. But there was definitely something about The Collector which set him apart. Spook had no difficulty aligning himself with a person of such immense presence. He dipped his head, just a little.

'So,' went on The Collector, 'how much rule bending might you be prepared to do . . . for eighty million?'

10

Spook stared at him. The Collector stared back, smiling and letting his question hang in the air.

Spook swallowed. 'Eighty million?'

The Collector nodded.

'Pounds? Dollars? Euros?'

'Pounds sterling,' said The Collector.

Spook let out a long breath and shrugged. 'It would still depend. What rules?'

'You remember the man Max and Kamilah so impressed last night? The one with the pretty girlfriend who got the diamonds from Max's first trick?'

Spook nodded. Mr Millionaire.

'What did you make of him? From where you were sitting?'

Spook shrugged. 'Not much. Arrogant. Rich . . .

Controlling,' he added, remembering how the girlfriend had sought his permission.

'Beautifully summed up,' said The Collector. 'Well observed. And what a transformation then, don't you think, from idle, bored, and dismissive to shocked, entranced, and fawning?'

Spook smirked. He could remember that extremely well. Had it not been Mr Millionaire's rude yawn which had finally provoked him to help Max?

'That was all your work, of course. And you achieved more than you know. Firaz Bahkar has invited Max and Kamilah—and their young technical assistant—along to a private dinner party, tomorrow night, at his villa overlooking the bay. Of course, Max will have to sing for his supper. Mr Bahkar wants his guests to be charmed and amazed by magic of the calibre he witnessed last night.'

'OK,' said Spook. 'But I'm guessing Max isn't getting an £80 million fee.'

'Sadly no,' laughed The Collector, adding quietly: 'I think we both know dear Max isn't quite in *that* league. Maybe one day, with your help . . . but not yet. There is a different way of realizing the £80 million. And that's where your talents will truly be put to the test, Spook. Of course, your help will be needed for the entertainment. But it's what happens after that which really interests me. What do you know about art, Spook?'

Again Spook shrugged. 'A little. I know Van Gogh from Picasso.'

'Useful,' said The Collector, glancing up and beckoning Max and Kamilah to sit down with them on the recliners. 'Because it's a Van Gogh we'd like to steal from Mr Bahkar's villa. With your help.'

Spook felt a slow tingle at the base of his spine and shook his head, smiling, as the tingle rose up towards his shoulders. 'You kidnapped me . . . so I can help you stage a *heist?*'

The Collector laughed. With energy and conviction. Max quickly joined in. 'You value yourself very cheaply, Spook,' said The Collector. 'One little heist? No—this is just a means to an end. My master plan, as you so endearingly name it, is far more than digging up a few score million. It's what we need the money *for* that really concerns you. Amazing times ahead, Spook. And to achieve the full potential of your powers we will need plenty of resources. Money needs to be simply not an issue. See tomorrow night as a small step towards your future. In years to come you'll barely remember it.'

Spook could think of nothing to say for a while. His insides were fizzing again. He would never agree to using his powers to become a common thief. It was beneath him. But an *un*common thief . . . ?

'What's the plan?' he said and Max, Kamilah, and The Collector all gave him identical smiles. Smiles which said 'He's in.'

They took him down to Max's room and spread a floor plan out on the table. It was of Firaz Bahkar's St Tropez villa, which was set high in the hills above the bay, commanding enviable views of the Mediterranean coast. There were glossy colour photos, too, of the interior. The villa was surprisingly small for a billionaire (as he now knew Bahkar to be) thought Spook—just five bedrooms with en suite bathrooms on the first floor and five rooms on the ground floor. A grand arched doorway led into the entrance hall with its sweeping marble staircase and floor. A doorway under the stairs led to a private cinema while off to the right of the hall lay a large entertaining room, also tiled with marble and fitted out with chandeliers, fine French antique furniture, a dining table long enough to seat twenty guests, and a high ornate fireplace. The single storey kitchen and staff quarters annex lay to the right of the entertaining room, through a covered walkway. But to the rear of the entertaining room, up three curved steps, lay a split-level chamber which was Bahkar's private art gallery. The photos showed pale walls covered with framed paintings, each artfully lit by suspended spotlights hanging from a grid of fine steel rods which criss-crossed the ceiling.

'I'm guessing this is where your interest lies,' commented Spook, prodding the gallery on the floor plan.

'Very astute,' said The Collector. 'Bahkar has an impressive gallery. He is obsessive about acquiring paintings with an insane price tag. In the late 1990s he managed to pick up Van Gogh's *Portrait of Doctor Gachet* for around a hundred million dollars—as far as anyone knows. Private collectors are notoriously shy of talking about money. There are two Doctor Gachets in fact—both Van Gogh. The other one is in the Musée d'Orsay in Paris— but this hasn't affected the price tag of Bahkar's.

His Doctor Gachet is now estimated to be worth at least a hundred and thirty million dollars—or around eighty million sterling.'

He slid a picture in front of Spook. It showed, in Van Gogh's characteristic brushwork of abundant yellows and blues, a red-haired man in a cap and a buttoned jacket, resting on one elbow with some books and greenery, gazing pensively out of the painting.

'OK,' said Spook. 'And . . . ?'

Max and The Collector exchanged looks.

'The gallery is, of course, very well protected,' said Max. 'Exterior and interior cameras, all wired individually on separate power feeds. The alarm is triggered by pressure sensors across the floor as well as a grid of randomly programmed laser sensors which scan the room—all running from a central computer locked in a titanium case under Bahkar's bed.'

'So—you short out the alarm . . . ' hazarded Spook.

'No.' Max shook his head. 'That would trip the system and set off a secondary alarm—connected directly to the St Tropez police, and, of course, Bahkar's private security people. And trust me, if you had to meet either . . . you'd want the police.'

'So—we've got the code . . . to switch it all off?' Spook asked, scanning the three faces around him. Kamilah giggled and shook her head.

'No. No code,' said Max. 'We won't need it.'

'OK.' Spook eyed them all with scepticism. 'So—a state of the art alarm system—you can't even breathe in the art gallery without tripping it.'

'And don't forget the steel shutter,' said Max. 'It rolls down every night, blocking the whole gallery off until the alarms are de-activated. You'd need an acetylene torch to burn through it—and even then it would take hours.'

'And yet you think we can steal his Van Gogh?' Spook rolled his eyes. 'With no code, no sabotage—just . . . what . . . help ourselves?'

'Almost,' said The Collector. 'There is one little flaw in Bahkar's security. His laser grid, unless he has noticed and reconfigured it in the past two weeks, does not entirely cover the room. There are two corners—here—and here,' he prodded at the bottom left-hand corner and the top right-hand corner of the gallery, 'where the lasers don't reach.'

'How do you know all this?' asked Spook, incredulous.

'Because I have observed it,' said The Collector. He waved away the *'How?'* which was forming on Spook's lips and went on, 'Now—these two golden triangles of opportunity are fifty-nine centimetres by forty by forty. *Just* big enough for you to stand in. And just big enough for Kamilah too.'

'But—how do we get there in the first place if there are lasers and pressure sensitive floors?' asked Spook. 'It would be insane to try. And even if we get to these safe triangles, how can we get back out again with the painting? You're all insane!'

'Easy, easy, son,' said Max, flicking anxious glances at The Collector, as if Spook really was his son and his responsibility. 'We've worked this out. It can be done. You *will* walk out with the painting and not only will Bahkar's men not stop you— they'll help you.'

'Truly, you're all certifiable.' Spook got to his feet. Nobody tried to stop him as he stalked out of the room and along the walkway. Outside the sweet sea air buffeted his face as he rested his arms along the rail and stared across the bay. His insides and his brain buzzed and flipped. He was nervous. Agitated. But . . . there was no point in denying it . . . excited too.

'No,' he told himself, out loud. There was *no way* he was going to risk his new-found freedom by getting into some madcap plan to rip off some oil sheik or whatever he was. If he ever went back to Fenton Lodge it couldn't be in the back of a high security van from Interpol. And that, of course, was even more absurd. Any country which caught him out thieving would surely work out who—and *what*—he was. And he would never see England again.

He felt, rather than saw, Kamilah arrive next to him. She didn't try to cuddle up to him but stood beside him and gazed out to sea. 'It's beautiful, isn't it?' she said, her accent a little thicker than usual.

'Hmmm,' he responded, not looking at her, but feeling another of those hot inner pings go off all the same.

'I never thought I would get to see such beauty,' she said. 'I never thought this world . . . was for me.'

'You didn't?' Spook glanced round at her, surprised. He'd taken her for a girl well used to luxury, like Lisa back at Fenton Lodge. Lisa had the air of someone who always got what she wanted and so, he had thought, had Kamilah.

Now, as Kamilah shook her head, he noticed that her eyes were glistening. 'If you'd met me two years ago, you would not even remember me,' she said, softly. 'You would not recognize me. I was . . . in a bad way. Poor. Very poor. I was a dancer . . . I had always thought . . . ' and now she took a step away from the rail, holding it with one hand and raising the other fluidly above her head while her arched foot marked a graceful ninety degree curve across the narrow strip of deck, ' . . . I would be a ballerina.' She smiled. A tight, bitter smile. 'But that . . . that was not the kind of dancing I did. Not in the end.'

She dropped her eyes to her feet and turned back to the rail and the sea and still did not look at him. 'Max saved my life,' she said. 'When he found me. I still don't know why. What he saw in me. I was . . . a mess. But he took me on and . . . changed everything. Money, you see. He had money. Not millions . . . but enough to take me on and clean me up and turn me into something . . . pretty.'

'Pretty?' said Spook. He touched her shoulder. 'You're *beautiful*.'

She turned to him and he pulled her close so she could smile up at him, the tears welling in her eyes like fine rain across the sun. *Dear God, you're doing it again*, he told himself. He did not have such thoughts about any girl! Well . . . possibly . . . but no. Even Mia didn't make him come over so wet and flowery.

'Help us, Spook,' she said. 'We need you. *I* need you. Be bold and brave and clever for me. I know you can. It may seem like we are rich already—but we're not really. Not enough. Once we have enough money we will be safe . . . from anything. We can go where we want and be . . . whoever we want to be.'

He'd made up his mind before she started kissing him.

11

'Shall I?' Max asked, deferentially. The Collector gave him a smile and a cool nod and settled back in his armchair, leaving Max the floor.

'First we will have dinner. Then we will perform,' said Max. 'We will astound and amaze, as we did last night—but—and this is important, Spook— we will not terrify anyone. We do not need any atmosphere of fear, do you understand?'

Spook nodded. Back in Max's room there was hot coffee on the table and an air of deep concentration from the people around it, although The Collector seemed a little remote, sitting back in his chair as if he was merely an observer.

'During our evening we will undoubtedly get taken around the gallery,' said Max. 'Bahkar loves to show off his treasures to guests, so you will have an opportunity to see the corners. The Van Gogh is dead centre of the back wall—you can't miss it. In fact . . . have a look at it now.' And Max pulled a large leather case out from under the table. He opened it on the carpet and extracted an elaborately scrolled gold oblong frame, seventy or eighty centimetres tall, and turned it to the table. Pensive red-haired Dr Gachet stared out from the frame.

Spook blinked. The picture looked . . . old . . . authentic. 'It could be the real thing,' he murmured. 'Although I wouldn't know, of course, not being a forgery expert.'

'It will be the real thing, thirty-six hours from now,' said Max. 'This is the replica we will be switching the original for.'

'How will we switch it?' asked Spook. 'If I carry that into the corner it's never going to fit inside the golden triangle, is it? The lasers will hit it and trigger the alarm!'

'No—we're not taking this into the house at all,' said Max. 'Now—shut up and listen and I'll explain everything. Close your eyes if it helps. I want you to visualize everything clearly. You too, Kamilah. Right . . . here we go . . .

'8.15p.m.—Max, Kamilah, and Spook—who will be going by the name of Mark—arrive at Bahkar's gate ready to set up for the show. Helped by Captain Devlin, they will be carrying some cases of props and a frame for the black backdrop to create a shielded area, as usual. The pathway to the house is steeply terraced, with ornamental shrubs and bushes growing thickly on the steeper slopes. While transporting the cases in, Kamilah slips and the case she is carrying slides down the terrace into the shrubs. Mark helps her to retrieve the case and they continue up the path to the house.

'8.20p.m.—At the house, Max, Kamilah, and Mark set up for the show while Devlin returns to the vehicle and drives back to the boat, leaving the invited guests behind.

'9p.m.—Guests arrive. A lovely time is no doubt had by all. A tour of the gallery by Bahkar will certainly occur. Max will play the part of a respectful amateur while Mark and Kamilah will pay scant attention, fascinated, as they are, with each other. It must be obvious that they are a besotted couple.

'9.30p.m.—Bahkar's chef is excellent. Eat, drink, and enjoy . . . but not too much. Kamilah and Mark need to stay sober and keep a slim belly.

'10.30p.m.—Time for the magic show. Max and Kamilah will perform their best tricks—and they will be *assisted three times across the show by Mark, their best kept secret. This must be carefully rehearsed. There can be no surprises for Max and Kamilah, no matter how tempted "Mark" may be.*

'11.15p.m.—with applause and murmurs of amazement still ringing in their ears, Kamilah and Mark discreetly break down and pack away the set while Max charms Bahkar and other guests with close-up magic.

'11.45p.m.—Devlin returns with the vehicle to collect the cases and Mark and Kamilah assist him in carrying them down to the car. After the last case is delivered, under the watchful eye of the security crew, Mark and Kamilah return alone to the villa, while Devlin minds the car, to say their goodbyes.

'11.50p.m.—having thanked their host, Mark and Kamilah pause to gaze into the art gallery one last time before they depart. They MUST station themselves in the arched entrance to the gallery, on the top step. Here, they will turn, with a clear path to the French windows which open onto the terrace and then . . . they will walk, hand in hand, through the doors, down the terrace and directly into the car—canoodling all the way. The car door will close and Devlin will drive them away. Max, meanwhile, has a few more drinks. Mostly lemonade, but guests will believe a fair amount of gin is in it.

'12.10a.m. Max leaves in a taxi, slightly the worse for wear.

'12.30–1a.m. Other guests depart and Bahkar's villa is closed up for the night.'

'OK,' said Spook, after a long pause. 'Got all that. And as far as I can tell, Kamilah and I are in the car with Devlin and Max is in the taxi, all of us heading back to the boat. What am I missing?'

Max grinned. 'I will be in a taxi. Slightly drunk and very memorable. I'll probably do a little close-up magic for the cabbie. And you and Kamilah will have departed with Devlin in the car.'

'But . . . ' prompted Spook.

'Neither of you ever left the villa,' said Max. 'You simply threw an illusion of both of you walking to the car—the sight-line will be clear and well lit. But you'll need to be holding a simultaneous illusion, too, Spook—something to cloak you and Kamilah from view until your doppelgängers are safely in the car and out of sight. Then you must, under cover of illusion, get to your corners for stage two.'

'Stage two,' repeated Spook, feeling the adrenalin surge through him.

Max smiled. ' . . . is where the fun *really* starts.'

* * *

'Do you really think we can do this?' asked Spook, amid a flurry of hot bubbles.

Kamilah smiled at him through a waft of steam and eased herself lower into the churning water. Her hair was piled up on her head in a messy knot to keep it clear of the hot tub and her eyes, behind mirror shades, gave nothing away. 'Of course,' she said, at length. 'It is well planned. It can be done.'

'*Can* be done,' said Spook, easing his own shoulders down under the water, wishing his chest was just a little broader and less pale, but careful to keep his left wrist, in its cast, elevated. The blue sky arched above them as they reclined in the hot fizzing pool on the upper sky deck. Everyone else was below deck—except The Collector who had silently departed yesterday and would not see them again until after the heist. It was good to be alone with Kamilah.

'Ninety per cent of our act is confidence, you know,' she said. 'Almost anyone can learn the tricks—but not everyone can carry them off. You need grace, timing, charm, sleight of hand . . . but most of all, confidence. You must have confidence about tonight, Spook.'

Spook was silent. Confidence. Hmmm. Not something he was usually in short supply of, but through the past twenty-four hours it seemed to have fled. He hadn't *said* anything, of course, but the truth was, he was sick with nerves. They'd gone shopping in St Tropez after lunch yesterday and Max had splashed out obscene amounts of money on clothes and footwear for him. Even on a Rolex watch. The trunks he was wearing now cost a hundred and twenty euros! Max said he was making up for lost time. But as delightful as it had been to be spoilt—for whatever reason (because he was still not convinced Max wasn't lying about the father business)—Spook couldn't fully enjoy it. His insides were clenched tight the whole time.

Kamilah took off her sunglasses and gazed at him. She raised five pretty toes to the surface and flicked some water in his face. 'Stop looking so serious, Spook!' she giggled. 'This is easy. We will be fine. And soon—very rich! And nobody will even know it was us!'

Spook tried to smile. Then he caught Kamilah's foot when she tried to splash him again, and ran his fingernails across the soft instep while she shrieked and giggled and squirmed out of his grasp. For some minutes he was able to stop thinking about the crime he was due to commit in a few short hours.

'Come on,' said Kamilah, at length, rising from the steam like a bikini-clad water goddess. She grabbed a fluffy white towel from the edge of the hot tub and threw it around her as she stepped out. 'Max wants to go through the act one more time, remember? And you have to promise not to scare me!'

Spook felt a surge of delight. He would never tire of scaring Kamilah.

And if he pulled off the heist tonight, with confidence and aplomb, she would be even more impressed. They would be bonded through their adventure. And he could sail on around the world with her for ever.

Max had a camcorder set up in the guest lounge on the main deck. He filmed the rehearsal—which was mostly a walk-through in which he and Kamilah paced the wide polished wood floor, outlining their moves in graceful mime and talking through the patter in a weird, low-key mutter. What they really wanted to rehearse was Spook's three illusions.

They had agreed that he would do his own version of the Zombie Ball—except his, of course, would not depend on fine steel rods and black felt sheets. His could hover anywhere in the room and move at any speed, in any direction. It could glow and pulsate and even change shape. 'As long as it's not frightening,' warned Max. 'You have to keep a close eye on the audience reaction, Spook. They have to believe it's an amazing trick—not a paranormal event.'

'Yes—you said. About six times,' said Spook, letting his Zombie Ball fade out.

The next illusion was to be similar to the 'rip in time and space' performance at Les Caves. Because, Max said, Bahkar would have told his guests all about it and would want it shown to them. Spook would leave out the wartime French bar visual, though, as it would have no relevance at the villa.

And finally, as a homage to Bahkar's homeland of Yemen, Spook would create a mesmerizing sand dune illusion, in which camels and desert snakes would rise from a sea of sand—an oasis mirage which would end in a whirling sandstorm before vanishing into thin air. Spook ran through the illusions with ease, idly fiddling with his new watch as he did so. When he'd finished, leaving Kamilah and Max speechless, he got up and shrugged. 'So . . . we're good to go?' he asked, with as much casual swagger as he could summon.

Max let out a long exhalation and then went, hands shaking, to the camcorder. He flicked a few switches on its control panel and then prodded a button on the wall behind him. A huge screen rolled down and a few seconds later Max was replaying the rehearsal across it. He looked tense. Spook smiled. He knew what Max was fearing— that the illusions could not be caught on camera. And it was a reasonable concern—after all, Spook was bending live human subjects to his will while creating his illusions. Something in his Cola brain was able to hook something in the audience brain—and force each person to see and even hear and—to some extent—feel his illusions. When his final flourish with the sand dune vision had ended in a whirling storm he could see Max and Kamilah's eyes narrowing and flinching, as if there was wind and sand blowing in their faces. There wasn't. There wasn't a breeze in the room—but something in their brains told them otherwise and they reacted exactly as if the sandstorm was real. And *they* knew it wasn't! It was as if their eyes, once convinced, quickly collaborated with the illusionist in convincing all the other senses to believe. Spook *loved* the human brain.

Max visibly relaxed when he saw the Zombie Ball on the camera's play back screen. Then a grin spread across his face. 'This . . . is going to be so amazing,' he said. He stared at Spook with a fanatical intensity. 'We are going to rock the world!'

Yes, thought Spook. *I am.*

12

The hardest illusion Spook had to pull off was of being calm. As the Mercedes people carrier wound around the hillside roads up to Bahkar's villa, his heart rate seemed to rise with every metre above sea level they climbed. When Kamilah took his hand it only served to make his pulse lurch along faster. He thought fleetingly of Mia. When she took his hand it filled him with warmth and calm. But she was a healer . . . of course that's what she'd do. For anyone. Spook shook his head when he thought of how he'd imagined he was in love with Mia. He knew now that those feelings were childish . . . just the result of the Mia Effect; the healer's aura of warmth and well-being which spread to everyone she met. What he was feeling for Kamilah now was much more intense. The real deal.

He took long slow breaths. He *had* to get calm. Centred. He'd faced far more perilous situations than this. It was a simple deception and theft from the kind of man who'd only care about losing the painting because of the dent to his ego. Bahkar would claim on his insurance and have another priceless work of art on the wall within a week. No—it wasn't guilt or any sense of danger that was making his blood pound in his ears—it was the horror of how he would feel if he didn't come up to scratch; if he didn't play his part well enough and the whole elaborate plan fell apart. He didn't think he could take it if Kamilah ever looked at him with disappointment, or worse, pity.

'You look good in black,' Kamilah murmured, still holding his hand. He had to agree. He was in a black silk shirt and tie and a black dinner suit. His shoes, although they looked like normal dress shoes, of shiny black leather, were in fact as supple as ballet pumps, with soft suede soles. He could move around in them in complete silence—that had been the point of Max buying them from a dance costumier's. Spook's hair was lightly waxed, lying in sculpted dark red waves across his head and glistening just slightly—exactly as he liked it.

His Rolex watch with its glinting gold bevel, sat upon his right wrist, as he was unable to secure it around the cast on his left. Even so, it looked as if it belonged. He was born to be rich and to wear wealth with style. The modest taste of wealth his father—Gordon Williams—had been able to supply, had merely quickened his appetite for more. He'd resented the boys at the boarding prep school he'd attended before the Cola power arrived, whose parents were living in bigger houses and driving more expensive cars. And he'd always planned to one day outdo them all. He wouldn't have to wait much longer.

Kamilah was also in black. She would perform tonight's show in what she had on—a short figure-hugging dress with black sequins scattered across the bodice and skirt. It was designed to be stretchy and easy to move in. Kamilah's shoes had lower heels than usual—silver dancers' sandals with a bendable mid-sole and suede under the toes and heels. Also silent to move in. They matched the silver chain choker and silver stars at her throat and ears. Her hair was pinned up, and little curls of it fell to her neck and across her high cheekbones. She looked spectacular, thought Spook, trying not to stare. He closed his eyes and worked on his breathing.

'Everything all right, son?' Spook's eyes sprang open to see Max leaning around from the front passenger seat.

'Fine,' he snapped. 'Stop calling me "son".'

Max grinned. 'You'll be happy about it one day.'

'What is your . . . adoptive father like?' asked Kamilah.

'He's not my adopt—oh, whatever!' Spook waved a dismissive hand. 'He's fine. A dad. He is . . . dad-ish.'

'Kept a firm hold on you when you were young, I bet,' said Max. Spook did not reply, so he went on. 'Bit of a military man, Gordon, yes? Likes everything shipshape. Ordered. Sensible. Practical. Unsentimental. Must have thrown his world into chaos when your Cola power emerged.'

Spook said nothing.

'How did you know?' asked Kamilah. She reached up and touched his cheek, gently guiding him round to look at her as the setting sun through the open Mercedes window flicked fingers of gold across her face and made her eyes glimmer like emeralds. 'How did it start?'

'At school,' said Spook. 'With a ghost.'

'A ghost?' She shivered with delight. 'You made people see a ghost?'

'Yes,' said Spook, a tight smile weaving across his mouth as he remembered. 'The boys in my dorm were talking about a ghostly caretaker—a man who was supposed to have hanged himself in the attic in the nineteenth century. And all of a sudden, there was old Greaves himself, shuffling down the lino between our beds, dragging a frayed noose in one hand, eyes all dead and black, moaning and croaking, with gory red rope marks cut into his neck . . . '

'Oh my God,' marvelled Kamilah, while Max watched intently, still leaning over the back of his seat as Devlin negotiated hairpin bends over breathtaking drops. 'What happened?'

'I nearly wet myself,' said Spook and Kamilah gasped and then giggled, pressing her fingers across her lips. 'I didn't realize what I was doing. Greaves had just stepped out of my imagination and I had no idea what had happened. As soon as the other boys started screaming and running for matron I panicked along with them and then it just disappeared. It was only later, after we'd all been calmed down and put back to bed, that I brought him back again. I was the only one awake that time . . . shivering under the sheets, trying not to scream. Then I realized that whatever I thought of . . . he did. I thought *left*—he walked left. I thought *right*—he walked right. I thought *stop*—he stopped. Then he skipped. Then he did a tap dance. Then he turned into a giant blancmange. I thought I was losing my mind.' He took a breath and ironed out the croak in his voice.

'How long did it take you to understand?' asked Max.

'A few days,' said Spook. 'First I was too terrified to try anything else. Then . . . when it was broad daylight and noisy and smelling of roast beef for lunch and as normal as it could be . . . then I would play. I tried a mouse. Running through the classroom and freaking out the geography teacher. That was . . . fun. Then—a cat. A big fat tabby, sitting on the windowsill outside maths, pawing at the glass until the teacher went to shoo it away. Then I'd try out bigger stuff. A car chase across the quad—the police got called for that one. A wild horse running amok across the tennis courts. RSPCA came out—but it had gone by the time they got there.'

'What next? What next?' breathed Kamilah.

'Nothing next,' said Spook. 'The government picked me up about five days after the first illusion—the ghost. They had to tell *me* what was going on. I had no idea what I was.'

'And how did Gordon take it?'

Spook was silent. Here was where his anecdotes ended. The look his father had given him, standing in the drawing room with two government officials, holding a crisp white form from Whitehall in one shaking hand and a pen in the other, would never leave him. Disappointment, disillusionment, disgust. All the Ds. And the biggest D of all. Disengagement. Gordon Spencer had snapped apart from him completely that day. He would, naturally, add Duty to the list of Ds. Spook was family, after all. Or was he? Now Spook saw that scene again with enlightened eyes. Had his father known he was *not* his father?

'Another time,' said Max. 'We're here. I need you both to focus now. In a few hours we will be on our way to Italy. Multimillionaires.'

The car had drawn up to a pair of high, wrought-iron gates set into posts of terracotta stucco, interrupting a wall which had to be four metres high. The wall, which curved in and out along Bahkar's sprawling hillside estate, was topped with a glittering forest of glass shards. Devlin got out of the car and pressed a button on the brushed steel panel on the left of the gates. After a few exchanges in French, the security camera on a post above the gates turned smoothly towards them and Max got out of the passenger seat to give it a cheery wave. There was another rattle of French from the grille on the brushed steel panel and then the gates slowly opened.

They drove through and paused as two suited security guards emerged from a hut to greet them. The men seemed reasonably friendly, although watchful, and were wearing showy headsets with coiled wires running from the comms in their right ears. They guided the vehicle to the far end of a gently sloping car park, paved with pale yellow herringbone brick. Six or seven cars were already parked here. Four fairly ordinary saloons, two red Lamborghinis and one dark grey Aston Martin. Spook stopped his mouth dropping open and told himself that a year or two from now, he would be driving an Aston Martin DB9 of his own. In emerald green.

The villa was set into a steeply terraced hillside, landscaped with exquisite Mediterranean planting to the front of the house and olive groves and vines on either side. As they climbed the steps, hauling the packing cases filled with props, the view of St Tropez bay uncurled below them, indigo blue as the sun marked a last fond streak of pink along the horizon. The lights of the waterfront glittered like diamonds. Spook pulled his gaze away from the view and focused on climbing the steps and steep paths to the house. Myriads of tiny paper lanterns were strung along the paths, and citronella candles on wooden stakes were planted among the shrubs and flowers, giving off a heavy lemon scent and keeping the mosquitoes at bay.

'Oh!' Kamilah gave a little exhalation of annoyance as her case slid out of her hands and bumped off the path into some flowering bushes. She laughed and scrambled down to retrieve it before Spook could turn to help, and seconds later she was back on the path behind him. Neither of the security guys, chatting with Max by the car, appeared to have noticed. Spook smiled to himself and climbed on up to the villa.

The villa was another typical St Tropez mini

palace with crimped red clay tiles along its roof, pale golden plaster walls and four wide archways across a courtyard leading to the entrance hall. It was exactly what Spook had been visualizing, with the help of the floor plan and the photos. A long, rectangular pond lay in the centre of the courtyard, stocked with koi carp, lily pads, and three small fountains.

They were welcomed into the entrance hall by three members of domestic staff, while the security guards peeled away and remained outside. The housekeeper and what appeared to be two waiters, dressed in white shirts, black trousers and black bow ties, guided them into the main entertaining space. At the far end of this large room they had cleared an area to be used for the show. Spook, Devlin, and Kamilah got down to building the stage set and positioning props behind the curtained backdrop while Max was borne away for an early evening drink with Bahkar.

As soon as the set was ready Devlin departed and they relaxed . . . as far as possible . . . taking glasses of champagne (nobody here seemed to drink anything else, thought Spook) from the waiters and reclining in seats laid out along the open patio windows. 'You can't drink it all, remember?' Kamilah said, holding up her glass of pale amber bubbles. 'No more than half. You have to be absolutely in control.'

Spook nodded, rolling his eyes. As if *one* glass of sparkling wine was going to affect him! But he put the glass down on a mosaic-topped table and watched Bahkar's guests arrive, climbing the terraces with laughter and excitement, dripping with expensive clothes and priceless jewellery.

'And don't forget,' said Kamilah, taking his hand. 'We're meant to be besotted.' She glanced at him teasingly. She must *know*, thought Spook, that it was no act for *him*. As the first four guests were shown into the room he decided it was a good time to fulfil his role and bent to kiss her. It was the first time he had ever made the move to kiss a girl—until now Kamilah had made all the moves and he'd just responded, mostly in shock. Now he fervently hoped his mouth would do what it was supposed to. And what that hell *was* it supposed to? He needn't have worried. Kamilah reached up and put her arms around his neck, taking control of the kiss with a giggle. After a couple of seconds she pulled away from him and coughed, sitting apart from him decorously, indicating that guests were in the room. Scene one. Kiss in front of guests. Done.

The guests were mostly in their thirties or forties—friends and acquaintances who moved in Bahkar's privileged world. The woman he'd been with at Les Caves was also there, wearing a shimmering midnight blue sheath of a dress and obviously very excited to see Max Carlyle again. Max returned from private drinks with Bahkar as the man arrived to greet his guests. After an hour of drinking and chatting, the moment Spook had been keenly anticipating arrived. Bahkar submitted to his guests' requests to see around the private gallery. It was easy and natural for Spook, Kamilah, and Max to join them. The gallery looked exactly as it had on the photos. Marble floor, pale walls filled with frames. Monet, Turner, Renoir, Degas—all fought for attention alongside the Van Gogh. And the Van Gogh looked exactly the same, down to every last detail of the frame, as the fake one he'd seen on the boat. Spook had a very good eye for detail and his memory was verging on photographic when it came to images. He wondered why Max and The Collector didn't simply sell the copy. But he guessed there were probably marks on the original canvas hidden by the frame which would indicate to an expert whether a painting was genuine or fake.

The guests were poetic and sycophantic in their appreciation of Bahkar's collection. *Such taste, such elegance. Such an eye* . . . It filled Spook with contempt for the man, whose oily skin and puffed-out chest made him look quite reptilian. Bahkar was not an ugly man but his expression of smug satisfaction was nauseating to behold. As was the way he glanced appraisingly at Kamilah, several times, despite his girlfriend's presence at his side, as if he'd like to acquire her too. Spook felt no qualm at all about stealing from him. Other Colas might have, but he understood exactly what The Collector meant when he had said 'We go by different rules'. He was not an ordinary person. He was a class above Bahkar and all his toadying guests.

He also rather liked the idea of building a reputation. The most astonishing high stakes burglar in the world . . . He would never be caught, of course, and he would always pull off the heists with style and aplomb. Maybe leaving some kind of calling card. Perhaps a Seven of Diamonds . . . What would they call him? The Cat? The Panther? The Shadow? Hmmm . . . he thought those had already been taken. He'd have to think on it.

Dinner seemed to last an eternity. There were five courses—each exquisitely prepared and deserving of all the murmurs of wonder from the diners—but Spook could barely eat anything. He hoped anyone who noticed would imagine he was just too preoccupied with Kamilah to think about eating. And that was partly true.

At last coffee and mints were served and the audience gathered at the far end of the room where twenty seats had been set out, a palpable air of excitement growing as the lights dimmed and the show began. Seated on the far end of the front row, Spook concentrated hard and went into his act. First the Spook Williams Zombie Ball . . .

He was even more pleased with his second show. Because this time he had known what was coming, he was able to plan and apply much more finesse to his illusions and work them seamlessly in with Max and Kamilah's real fakery. The Zombie Ball, zooming around like a tiny UFO, had the audience open mouthed from the start—and immediately doubly receptive to Max's tricks. They were *so* suggestible, it was all Spook could do not to laugh out loud as Max went through his act. The tricks that had them agape and applauding were often the simplest to explain—with false panels and dropping mirrors and the most basic misdirection. If any one of these sheep actually looked properly at what was happening it should be obvious how the trick was done. But they didn't. They looked only at the shiny things . . . never the dark and dull. And in the dark and dull parts was where the magic was truly pulled off. Spook had read an article on Derren Brown—someone he truly admired—in one of his magazines. Brown had said that learning a trick was one thing, but in order to be a true success as a magician, you had to make it beautiful. And he didn't mean sexy female assistants. It was in the delivery, the theatre, the connection with the audience.

Although he had grudging respect for Max's sleight of hand and his obvious experience, Spook saw nothing beautiful in the man's performance. He was cheesy. A holiday camp act who'd managed to make the big time in the nineties when people were less sophisticated. Max would never cut it now if he hadn't already had some early fame to trade on. Kamilah was in another league, of course . . . she couldn't help it that she'd taken work with Max. It was clear that she'd been desperate.

The audience were utterly charmed when he reprised the rip in space and time and featured some of them inside it. But they were on the edge of panic when he brought back the velociraptor. Max shot him a swift glance and Spook reined the illusion in fast—helped also by Bahkar standing and applauding and singing out, 'See! I told you I would amaze you!' to all his guests as if he had created the illusion himself.

The finale, with the sand dunes, left them all gasping with wonder. And it was beautiful too, thought Spook, especially as the sand camels and the sand snakes slowly intertwined and became a whirling sandstorm before drifting away in spiralling ribbons and dissipating beneath a cloudless Yemeni sky framed in a doorway against Max's black felt backdrop. Spook knew he really had outdone himself. Everyone was frozen in their seats, staring with rapt amazement, mouths open, hands gripping chair arms—one or two were even crying!

To say the evening was a success was a gross understatement. The guests fell over themselves to get to Max and congratulate him as soon as he'd returned to them. Kamilah was also plagued by fawning people desperate to know the secret of the show, but she smiled winningly at them and made her way back to Spook for a big congratulatory hug.

'Do you work on the show too, young man?' asked a busty middle-aged American woman, her eyes shining.

'Yes. I'm Mark—Max's technical assistant,' said Spook, dropping his eyes modestly.

'So you know how it's all done!' The woman stared at him in awe. 'Come on . . . you can give me a little hint, can't you?' She smiled roguishly at him. 'I'd love you all to come and do my daughter's birthday party in California. I'd make it *seriously* worth your while . . . ' She winked at him. 'So come on . . . how's it done?'

Spook smiled politely at her, his arm around Kamilah. 'It's highly skilled, practised and thought through,' he said. 'Max has been working on his act for years. And . . . of course . . . some of it is, genuinely, magic . . . '

'Oh, pshaw! You!' The woman dug him with a chubby, diamond-heavy finger and patted her lacquered blonde hair. 'You and your Magic Circle! I guess you just can't tell me the truth.'

Spook smiled again and allowed Kamilah to lead him away.

'Better get used to that,' she said, softly, wrapping her arms around him. 'Are you ready for the main show? It won't be long now.'

Spook nodded. Creating the illusions had bolstered his courage a lot. He felt incredibly powerful. He could do anything . . . anything at all.

13

On the stroke of midnight, like Cinderella, Spook and Kamilah departed from the ball.

The guests, Bahkar, Max, and his staff were dotted randomly around the large entertaining room and as they climbed the steps to the empty gallery, Spook and Kamilah, hand in hand, turned to look across the party, out to the terrace and down the hill. They could easily make out the path to the car park as it was lit all the way with the fairy lanterns and citronella candles. Devlin was clearly to be seen, from their elevated position on the top step, leaning on the open passenger door, where they'd left him as they'd delivered the last of the cases of props and deconstructed set, five minutes ago.

Spook squeezed Kamilah's hand in warning and then worked the double illusion. He felt a cold spot in his solar plexus as his focus narrowed down to laser-like precision. He could almost *see* the walls and the gallery view behind him; he'd spent many minutes building up the image in his mind across the evening. Now, pulling the cloak of that image across Kamilah and himself, he let the second illusion kick in. He and Kamilah, as far as anyone watching would ever know (and he included the security cameras discreetly lodged above the chandeliers) now stepped down and walked across the marble floor towards the open patio doors.

Spook, focused as he was, still felt a lurch of alarm as the busty American woman suddenly trotted after his phantoms with enthusiastic intent, flapping her hands agitatedly. *Dear God, she was going to harangue him for the 'secrets' again!* He made phantom Spook give her a friendly little wave and speed up, but she wasn't to be put off.

'Wait—wait, young man! Remember, I wanted to book you all for my daughter's party!' she called, speaking in a slightly slurred voice. She'd been quaffing champagne all evening.

'Then it's probably *me* you need to talk to,' said Max, moving at speed and intercepting her before she could grab phantom Spook's arm and stagger backwards in shock when her fingers passed right through it. With only a flicker of a glance towards the stairs where his accomplices stood like rock, Max led the woman away, charming her one to one so that she didn't even look back. The phantoms smiled and waved to the assembled crowd, most of whom were not paying them much attention, and then stepped out into the courtyard, skirted the formal pond and walked down to the terrace.

Spook gave Kamilah a gentle push beside him and she edged away slowly to the far side of the archway which led into the gallery. In case anyone decided to take another look at the paintings, or one of Bahkar's discreet security guys did a check, they needed to be off the main path. His gaze never wavered, though, from the phantoms he was sending down the terrace. He had to hope nobody else would try to catch up with them—yet, at the same time, they needed to be seen.

Already Devlin was giving them a wave from the car and opening the rear passenger door. Thirty seconds more and the phantoms would be in the car. Spook risked a little smooch, on the last terrace above the car park, smiling to himself and glancing at real Kamilah, who was still visible to *him* despite his illusion. It was complex . . . but he could do it. He was the best. He could even allow her to see *him*. She smiled back at him with a wink.

The phantoms got into the car and Devlin carefully closed the door, hiding his passengers behind mirror windows. He got into the front seat, waved genially to the security guard who opened the electric gates, and ten seconds later he, the car full of props, and the illusory young couple, were gone.

Spook nodded to Kamilah and they turned and stepped silently into the gallery. He went left and made his way to his golden corner and she crossed to the right and stepped into hers, diagonally opposite. Before she rested her back against the wall she undid the black sequined bodice of her dress, unclipping a series of hooks and eyes down the front and revealing a rigid black basque underneath. Spook averted his gaze and then laughed to himself. She couldn't see him now anyway. And besides, this was no striptease. Kamilah knew exactly what she was doing. She reached under her skirt now, and withdrew a bag, made of silk-like material which was far stronger than it looked, with narrow cord straps and nylon clips. Slinging the bag over her back and pulling the cords tight over her shoulders, Kamilah took a deep breath, glanced from the ceiling to the floor, pushed her heels into the corner and turned out her toes before pressing her back firmly up to the two walls that met at ninety degrees behind her shoulders. She held her arms straight down, close to her body, closed her eyes as if meditating, and began to wait.

Spook, without any unhooking or bag retrieval needed, copied her stance, making his form as slim and compact as possible. 'If you slouch,' Max had warned them earlier, 'or let your belly bulge out a little after eating too much, you'll blow it. There is no room—literally—for error. You find your corner, you fit into it, and you stay still.'

Staying still was harder than hé had imagined. Across the room Kamilah seemed fine, as if she had settled into some kind of trance. Then, of course, she would have done this kind of thing before. She could fit into boxes and trunks and sliding cabinets which appeared to slice her into three parts. A lot of the brilliance of Max's show was down to Kamilah's lithe gymnastic ability and slender form. Magician's assistants slouched or put on a couple of pounds at their peril. Some had sustained nasty injuries from swords and sharp sheet blades by just slightly losing their figures or their suppleness.

How long now? he wondered. He didn't dare look at his watch as he focused on the double illusion. Kamilah's end was fine, but his own was harder. Maintaining a disguise illusion was never easy.

The sound of the guests was thinning out. There were definitely fewer people. It shouldn't be too long now. Max had set their minds at ease earlier that day, after the last rehearsal. 'Bahkar is a man of habit,' he'd said. 'He loves to play the host but he gets bored very easily and rarely allows guests to stay much beyond midnight. They are usually sent packing in time for him to retire to bed around one a.m. He likes to rise early for the stock markets and rarely changes his routine.' Spook fervently hoped Max's information was accurate. Holding himself still was also peculiarly tiring; he knew he mustn't even move his toes inside his shoes. He was glad he'd eaten little and drunk less. His insides were churning enough as it was. Kamilah, a beautiful statue in the opposite corner, seemed the epitome of calm. Her eyes were still closed. Did *she* feel calm? Was *she* completely confident of what she had to do?

He heard even less chatter now. And then Max's laugh rattled loudly through the room below. 'Aaaah, yes, you see—they've taken all the cases and gone ahead without me!' he said and Bahkar laughed.

'They leave the master magician behind?' said their host. 'Too keen to be alone, yes?'

'Yes,' agreed Max with a rueful laugh and a slight hiccup. 'Young love, eh? Well . . . there's my taxi. I'll let you get your sleep now, Firaz. Thank you for your invitation—it's been a most enjoyable evening.'

'You will come again,' stated Bahkar.

'When I am able,' said Max. 'We sail tomorrow. Many engagements!'

'You will come again. I will pay you double!' said Bahkar, sounding a little drunk himself. 'You are worth double . . . triple! The best magician I have ever seen. One day . . . you will tell me how you do it . . . '

'Maybe, one day,' said Max. 'Goodnight! Goodnight! Goodnight!'

Now Spook knew the guests were gone. Max had fulfilled his promise to say 'Goodnight' three times as a signal to Spook and Kamilah that he was the last to leave. Ten minutes later the staff were gone, taking the empty glasses and bottles with them. Five minutes after that the lights went off. Two minutes later there was a grinding metallic noise as the steel shutter rolled down, sealing the wide arch between the gallery and the room below. It locked with a heavy clunk across the floor.

Spook gulped and steadied himself. There was no turning back *now*.

Then the lasers came on.

14

Even though he'd been fully prepared for this, a jolt shot through him and his heart pounded so forcefully in his chest Spook feared that this alone would set off the motion sensors under his feet.

The red lasers swayed and danced hypnotically across the room, marking abstract patterns around the floor. At first it was so dark that these crimson needles were all Spook could see. He couldn't believe that Kamilah could possibly do what she was meant to do. She would never be able to see.

But as time passed his eyes adjusted and he began to make out the shapes of the many frames on the walls, lit randomly by passing lasers and also by the dim LED security camera lights beside the archway. Waiting was now the hardest thing. Here, in such low light he could let the illusion relax a little;

he could just project shadows rather than well-lit reality. This was a relief, but simply standing here, motionless, doing nothing, was almost unbearable. His head was swimming from all the effort and now a new horror grabbed at his throat. What if he just fell over? Keeping his balance amid the disorientating dance of the lasers was a challenge in itself. Now that he was no longer focusing so hard on the double illusion his head pounded and panic started to rise up in him. He began to feel extremely stupid when he thought now about his earlier fantasies of being a world renowned burglar. This was terrifying. He was going to faint or vomit and ruin everything, right here in front of Kamilah.

Click. A flare of blue-white light shot out across the room. Quickly, Spook threw dark between it and the two security cameras—an opaque dark which still allowed the lasers through. *Damn, he was good!* It would only show up as a blip—a flare caused by a technical glitch. Assuming anybody had been watching it at all. Simply doing this knocked the panic back down to a manageable level. Beneath the shield of his illusory darkness, Kamilah's torch glowed through the lasers. She was still tightly within her safe corner, looking up, her face eerily uplit, eyes dark and wide and focused. Moving her hands carefully up her body, taking care to keep her elbows tucked in safely, she first attached the torch, a small halogen light on a band, to her forehead. Then, pausing as a laser passed within three centimetres of her nose, she began to slowly maneouvre around the basque. A few seconds later a shining silver line appeared, moving up telescopically past her throat and nose and forehead until it was high above her head like a radio aerial. It continued upward, heading for the ceiling, until it reached the grid of metal lighting struts. Now it curled over, like the hook of a walking stick, its lower end still anchored in Kamilah's basque. Kamilah, keeping her eyes on the laser field, eased a wheel-shaped gadget out from her skirt and held it tightly in her right hand, while her left reached flatly for her belly.

'Are you ready?' she whispered.

'Yes,' whispered back Spook, utterly fascinated with watching her.

'Remember—don't move. Not yet. Me first. Here we go.'

Kamilah pressed a button on her bodice and

suddenly rose up from the floor, riding the rappel device to the ceiling in a smooth, controlled glide. The moment her feet left the floor the pressure sensors were tripped and a deafening bell sounded. Spook cried out in shock, even though—again—he had known this was going to happen. Letting his shock out of his mouth seemed to stop him lurching, though, so it was a good option. And anyway, Kamilah could not have heard him over the alarm, which was so loud it was making his head buzz. She was now up on the ceiling, wrapping her slim legs around the lighting rig and attaching the circular gadget to the rappel wire, where it connected to the steel strut.

Shouts and the sound of running feet on the marble floors echoed in to them in spite of the clanging alarm. A few seconds later the metal shutter began to rise, letting a wide blue column of light rise up with it. Kamilah switched off the torch on her forehead and hung still in the darkness, a metre above the nearest painting. She was impossible to see at first, but now, as one of the security guys crouched down, waving a gun into the room, the lasers abruptly switched off and normal lighting flooded on. Spook could make out her form, motionless, against the ceiling. By the time the shutter had fully risen, three men stood on the other side, armed and riveted on the gallery. Spook, though, had applied his illusions again and nothing could be seen of Kamilah . . . or of him.

The guards strode into the room, looking in all directions, and then at each other. At the centre of the gallery was a Greek sculpture, on a plinth. Spook, keeping his camouflage and Kamilah's firmly in place with his peripheral vision, glanced down and worked on his third simultaneous Cola trick. From the far side of the plinth a brown rat ran out, squeaking and shuffling as if it was lame.

The men spun round to stare at it and then burst out laughing as it shot across the room, out past the archway and down the steps. 'Un rat! C'est un rat, notre cambrioleur!' guffawed one of them, chasing across the room and making as if to gun the rodent down. The men visibly relaxed and murmured to each other, shaking their heads, and although Spook couldn't easily understand them—at least one was talking in Arabic, he thought—the gist was easy to get. 'All of this fuss . . . thanks to a rat!'

Then they holstered their weapons and left the room without once glancing up to the ceiling, where Kamilah still hung, swathed in the mirage of dimness, or across to the corner where Spook stood behind his self-projected camouflage.

The minute they had left the room, their footsteps and jocular remarks echoing back across the marble floors, Kamilah was on the move. She adroitly slipped the wheel gadget onto the metal strut of the lighting rig and looped the metal rappel hook over it, and then pulled herself smoothly along to the point where another strut crossed the first, ending her path of travel in that direction. Happily, this was just above the Van Gogh. Kamilah knocked a clip on the pulley, securing her steady on the strut. Then the lights went out. If The Collector's information was correct, the pulsing amber light on the LED high in the corner meant they now had two minutes before the lasers were switched back on. 'Two minutes,' hissed Spook, glancing down at his watch and still not daring to move his feet. The under-floor motion sensors could already be back on; there was no obvious way of telling. He knew that the shutter would follow next and then the lasers would be back.

Kamilah did not answer. She switched on her head torch and then pressed the button on her bodice and slid gently down, suspended on the rappel, her feet a metre above the floor. Turning gently in the air, she reached under her skirt again. Spook grinned as he saw the garter fixed tightly around her left thigh. She slid a small silver screwdriver from it and went to work at speed on the wall fixings of the Van Gogh frame. Spook had at first imagined that the paintings were simply hung on hooks, as in most homes—but of course these were much more carefully affixed. Kamilah swiftly unscrewed the fixings on either side of the painting.

Spook was beginning to get jittery again. He could do nothing to help. He would trigger the under-floor motion sensors again if he moved and they needed more time. Kamilah now placed her feet on the wall on either side of the painting, slid the screwdriver back into her garter and then eased the painting up, off another hook at its back and away from the wall. Spook felt a thrill run through him. She was really going to pull this off! Now she reached backwards over her head, tilting the frame and working it into the top of the bag across her back. Spook counted down, thirteen seconds, twelve, eleven, ten . . . Kamilah wrestled with the frame, breathing hard. It was so elaborately scrolled it was catching in the mouth of the bag. Nine, eight, seven . . . it still wasn't in. Six—she gave it a hard shove and it slid, with a tiny, muted thunk, into the bag, making her shoulders jar back and her feet lose contact with the wall.

With a hum and a rattle the shutter slid down, blotting out the light from the rooms beyond.

'Five seconds!' hissed Spook.

Kamilah twisted another button on her bodice and dropped to the floor, landing with springy knees, like a dancer, before straightening up. She reached above her and sent the dangling rappel wire gliding back along the strut to the far corner where its journey had begun. Then she turned to face Spook with a satisfied smile. He wanted to grab her and kiss her into next week. But he stayed still for a moment, waiting for her to catch her breath. 'Here they come,' he said. 'Ready?'

'Are you?'

He nodded.

The lasers cut right across Kamilah's smiling face.

15

Kamilah only beamed more, and her eyes sparkled in the red light for a second before flinching as the alarm burst into shrill life again.

'Best move here now,' said Spook, stepping closer to the edge of the archway and indicating that she do the same on the opposite side. The floor sensor alarm had also been turned on again at the same time, it seemed, because it began to shriek the moment Spook moved, working in awful disharmony with the laser alarm. Spook's legs shook. They had been set like rock for the past half an hour, with adrenalin pouring through them, and now they were barely able to hold him up. He took long, slow breaths, trying to ignore the freaky crimson needles of light dissecting his skin and the brain-splitting racket. Footsteps and annoyed shouts sounded outside. He pulled his focus tight on either side of the archway, cloaking himself and Kamilah in replicas of the walls behind them. And most importantly, creating a perfect temporary facsimile of the Van Gogh on the wall.

The shutter rattled up again, and again the three guards peered in under it, weapons cocked, hissing urgently to each other. And again, they found nothing amiss at first glance. Second glance, however, showed them the single fine metal wire of the rappel, dangling from the corner. Shouts rose among them and then one began to urgently work around the room, seeking other clues, while the other two fled out into the room below, throwing the brilliant chandelier lights on and searching for the intruder.

Spook and Kamilah, though, were already gone. Holding her hand, Spook could create a running shadow mirage to keep them both safe, but he knew the Van Gogh illusion would vanish at any time. And that wasn't really a problem. Out on the terraces it was easier. Even with light now flooding from the villa there was plenty of shadow thrown by the shrubs, bushes, and cypress and bay trees as they ran silently for the gates. Trying to contain his breathing, while his lungs threatened to burst through his ribcage, Spook led Kamilah to the sentry box by the gate. A guard was in it, bellowing down the phone line and looking wild-eyed as he took in the news from the villa.

As he finished with the call, Spook thrust Kamilah towards the electric gates and threw a blanket of wrought-iron illusion across her. She waited, the Van Gogh still securely on her back, as Spook brought Bahkar down the steps from the villa. The multi-millionaire was in pyjamas and a silk robe, wearing nothing on his feet, calling out in angry, unintelligible Arabic and gesturing clearly that the gates should be opened. The security guard, looking alarmed and disconcerted, jerked into the sentry booth and punched a button on a console below a TV screen. And then the electric gates began to open. They moved agonizingly slowly, but Kamilah wrapped herself around the edge of the opening three seconds later, snagging £80million worth of paint and canvas briefly against it, and then vanished into the darkness of the hillside road. Spook held his sight line as he too backed towards the opening gate. In thirty seconds he'd be away free too.

And then Bahkar came out of the villa. The *real* Bahkar, tearing across the steps and bellowing at the bewildered gatehouse guard who stood frozen over the gate security console, his eyes flitting back and forth between the real man and his doppelgänger. Spook let the illusion drop and turned to run.

But the guard had already hit the CLOSE button on the gates and they were gliding shut again. *NO!* Spook flung himself headlong for the narrowing gap between the high metal panels. He was too late. With a dull reverberation the gates closed and five instant deadlocks clicked into place. Spook's heart tripled its speed and his bladder threatened to lose all control. He was trapped!

He turned right and ran along the perimeter wall, hearing more shouts and volleys of French and Arabic. Bahkar was clearly in a state of outraged fury. They must have seen that the Van Gogh had gone by now. Thank God Kamilah had got away with it. She would be halfway down the hillside by now, and about to rendezvous with Devlin in a hire car. Bahkar might have the police already on the way, of course, and she might get caught . . . he could no longer protect her.

But then, as he stumbled along the perimeter

wall, his arms and legs getting snared and scratched by thorny bushes, he heard a shout. A different kind of shout. In spite of his fear and pain he let a bitter smile out across his mouth. They had found the Van Gogh. Dropped, in just a soft felt wrap, into the shrubbery halfway down the terrace path. The burglar, they would deduce, had failed and simply cut and run. It might be hours, days . . . even weeks before they discovered that it was a fake. This was what Kamilah had dropped on the way up to the villa earlier that evening, through the spring-loaded panel in the bottom of the case.

'This job has to be self cleaning,' Max had told them, so many hours ago, back on the boat. 'We will have long gone by the time the first alarm goes. Watched out of the grounds by the guards and, in my case, all the way back to the boat by a taxi driver. There will be nothing left behind to connect the burglary with Max Carlyle or his crew.'

Nothing left behind? Spook's bitter smile dropped off his face. Well . . . there was *one* thing left behind. 'Mark'—Max's useful young assistant.

'*Keep calm. Keep calm. Keep calm,*' Spook told himself, with every snatched breath. He had to think. He had to *think*. How was he to get out?

Three independent beams of torchlight were now tracing the grounds, edging away from the terrace lights, which had been switched back on, and towards the darker edges by the perimeter wall.

He did not fear discovery *now*. He was certain that he would easily be able to dodge the torchlight, staying shielded within shadow and illusion. But what then? He needed to get out. If he could not and was forced to hole up somewhere within Bahkar's grounds—which weren't all that extensive—sooner or later he would fall into exhausted sleep and any protecting illusion would fade.

There was a tall dark shape up ahead. A cedar tree, towering above the perimeter wall, but set back some four or five metres from it. Its branches, though, stretched out as far as the perimeter. It might be possible to climb the tree and edge out across the branches and drop to the other side of the wall. It was quite some drop . . . but perhaps the branches would bend down a little, taking away some of the height. He might have to wait it out in the tree for a while—allow the initial search to finish and the villa to calm down again and then go for it before dawn broke. More shouts sounded nearby and torch beams intersected further along the wall. There was no time to work out any other plan. Spook hurled himself at the cedar, grabbing handholds in its trunk, thankful for the grip of the suede soles of his dancer's shoes but cursing his awkward wrist cast. He reached the first branches within a minute and then froze. Keeping as still as he had in the gallery, he wove the illusion of dark branches and foliage around him. For now, at least, he was safe. He rested his forehead against the trunk and felt the pressure of his blood surging through his ears. How had this happened? Everything had been perfect. Perfect! They had carried out their plan to the letter! How could he have known, though, that the *real* Bahkar would arrive in the very place he was throwing an illusion of him?

Torch beams travelled the ground below and shone up into the tree for a few seconds. Spook held his breath and gripped the branches but he knew his illusion would hold. There would be no reason for anyone to climb up. He felt the light swipe his face and there were muted words below him—but no excitement. No shout of recognition, followed by warrior cries.

The torch beams had swung away and he smirked to himself. He was *good*. And then his heart froze and his blood seemed to chill and stand still in his veins. From up by the villa came a harsh, repetitive cry. A sound that made him think of Dax Jones, the shapeshifter Cola who had so infuriated him for the past few years with his resistance to glamour and his smug certainty that he really was *it*. Spook screwed up his face and gritted his teeth as terror began to knuckle its way into his chest. At last he and Dax Jones had something in common.

Now they both knew how it felt to be hunted by dogs.

16

Spook remembered how he had gloried in Dax Jones's panic attacks. The boy had been cornered, while in fox form, during a hunt. Spook knew this, because he'd been there. He was one of the foot followers that day. He loved the excitement of the chase, the guttural baying of the hounds, the vicious thrill of the kill. And he'd nearly seen Dax Jones dragged out of an abandoned fox's earth and ripped to shreds in front of him.

In the end, Dax had been saved and, in fact, Spook had reluctantly helped with that. But he'd had no end of fun at Dax's expense when they'd both returned to the college soon after. Dax had turned panicky and word got round . . . so Spook thought he'd 'help out' by bringing a fox hound into the college to see if Jones couldn't work through his issues. The boy had nearly wet himself in terror. And it had been the funniest thing Spook had ever witnessed, even if Darren had seriously— for the first time since they'd met—had a go at him. Darren was a soft hearted idiot, of course, but Spook hadn't wanted to lose the only friend he'd made, so he'd not wound Jones up about it again.

He'd loved having that bit of knowledge over Jones, though . . . having been there to see him nearly torn apart and then nobly throwing an illusion to get the hunt off his back so Jones could escape, had made him feel superior. And he'd treated Dax Jones's fears with derision and contempt. Part of him knew that this situation, then, was quite poetic. If Jones knew what he was facing now, he'd be punching the air and hooting with laughter. Or maybe not; Jones took everything—and himself—far too seriously. But Spook understood the hollow horror of it now, and knew there was nothing remotely funny in it. He was probably only two minutes away from discovery by hounds himself. There was nothing he could do to disguise himself. Even if his illusion worked on them—and he knew it wouldn't—they would still be able to smell him.

Spook stared along the branches towards the perimeter wall, fear tightening a cord around his throat as the baying grew louder and two more torch beams moved jerkily down through the terraces towards his hiding place. The branch very nearly reached the wall. If he could get to the end he might be able to jump. But what was on the other side? More lush Mediterranean vegetation, he hoped. A fall into that would be survivable—would give him a chance to roll, pick himself up, and run. And what was the alternative? Dog attack? Capture? He saw himself being dragged away by local police and then being identified and picked up by Interpol and then . . . revealed as a Cola to the French government which already knew far too much about what Colas could do to ever let him go.

Spook crawled along the branch, oblivious to the scrapes and punctures he was picking up from its twigs, as fast as he could. The branch held up well until he was halfway along it, and then began to sway and bend with his weight. The cast on his left wrist protected him from some of the minor wounds his right was getting, but made it awkward to grasp the smaller branches and twigs as he moved along. The dogs began to howl now, scenting him and pulling urgently against their leads. The men shouted to each other in excitement, understanding that their quarry was within reach. Spook scrabbled harder along the branch, close enough to the perimeter to see the top of the wall glinting in the moonlight. It was now or never.

Launching himself forward from his knees, it wasn't until he was in mid-air, arms outstretched, that Spook remembered why the perimeter walls glinted along the top. And there was no time to do anything about it. As his chest and arms cannoned into the wall and his legs scrabbled for purchase, a shriek of pain burst from his mouth. He was punctured over and over by the shards of broken glass. They lacerated his chest, arms, and hands as he slid back down off the wall. He landed heavily on his back, winded and gasping with shock and agony as warm blood welled up from scores of wounds and soaked into his black silk shirt and jacket.

Five seconds later the first dog found his throat.

17

Spook threw up his arms and tried to fend off the snarling Dobermann, feeling its teeth snagging into his neck and its hot breath puffing behind. Another hound seized his already bloody right forearm. Both dogs were shrieking with primeval canine delight and behind them Spook could vaguely hear shouting.

He was helpless. He couldn't summon any help from his illusions if he tried; his brain was spinning with random thoughts as he prepared to die: the boat, Kamilah, Max, The Collector, Fenton Lodge, Darren and Mia . . . Mia came last, smiling and running her palms across his face as if to prepare him kindly for the hereafter. A sob broke out through his screams as he thought of Mia.

'*Lâchez! Lâchez!*' he heard one of the guards

bellowing and there was a tearing of the skin under his chin as the hounds were wrenched off him and held back, whining, in check.

He lay, awash with blood, unable to move. One guard dragged the dogs, whining and reluctant, away while two others remained.

'*Il est mort?*' came another voice.

'*Non!*' replied the first. And he felt an exploratory kick against his hip.

'Get up!' said the man, staring down at him with contempt. Spook gaped at him. Get up? Get *up*? He was *dying*!

'Oh—so—it's the magician's assistant!' the guard added, his words heavily accented. His face was dim in the light but Spook could see a moustache and sneer under it. 'Bet you can't magic yourself out of this one, can you?'

There was a further exchange in French and the men obviously decided to take him back to the villa for further questioning. They made noises of disgust as they hefted him to his feet, realizing that he was drenched in blood.

'Not such a clever idea, was it, trying to steal from Bahkar?' muttered the one with the moustache. His colleague did not seem to speak English.

Spook said nothing.

'So—you were all in on it, were you?' grunted the man, as he and the other guard dragged him along.

'No,' gasped Spook, thinking of Kamilah. 'That idiot Carlyle couldn't pull off a burglary if you gave him the entry codes and a swag bag. I plan all his tricks for him. He's a simpleton.'

'Well, you didn't do so well yourself, did you?' smirked the guard. 'You had to drop your prize and run.'

Spook just grunted with pain. They were tightly grasping his upper arms, careless of his wounds. Blood was dripping from the tear in his neck, but he realized that if the dog had hit the artery it would be spurting out like a fountain. It looked as if he would live after all. He had got at least *that* lucky.

'Well, I can't wait to see what Bahkar does with you,' went on the guard as they neared the gatehouse where another guard was waiting, agog to see who the captive was. 'He does not like to lose sleep. It puts him in a *very* bad temper.'

'Where are the police?' mumbled Spook.

'Police? Oh . . . I don't think we need to bother the

police,' said the guard. 'It's much less complicated to deal with you ourselves. Less messy all round.'

Spook felt fresh dread spiral up through him.

'Bahkar is a man who guards his reputation,' smiled the guard, his eyes cold in the glow of the car park lights. 'He would not like it known that some youth barely past puberty got even as far as his garden with his favourite Van Gogh.'

'You're going to kill me,' stated Spook, in disbelief.

'After we've found out all about you,' grinned the guard. 'Magic yourself out of *that* if you can.'

Spook's head began to spin again. He had powers. He had huge, unfathomable *powers*. How could he be trapped like this? He was a Cola. He was one of Britain's most precious assets! How could his life end like this?

Behind him there was a low electronic hum and voices. Twisting round he saw the gates opening and two more security guards entering. Clearly they had been searching the other side of the wall in case he'd managed to scale it. Spook's heart hammered painfully inside him. It was now or never. Turning back to the villa he dragged together every last ounce of energy and pulled his focus in tight. This was going to need to be good. Incredibly good.

A moment later the villa exploded in a titanic ball of flame. Plaster and brick and shattered windows flew in all directions. The pulse through the air was tremendous. Beyond it he could hear the screams of the guards around him as they instinctively threw themselves to the ground, covering their heads, cringeing against the avalanche of blazing rubble blasting directly at them.

Spook lost no time at all. The electronic gates were already closing, completely unaffected, of course, by the phantom catastrophe. He ran for it, sliding sideways through the narrow gap only seconds before the gates clanged shut and reverberated with sealed locks. Spook did not stop to catch his breath on the far side of the gates. He turned and fled down the dark hillside, stumbling as fast as he could into the cover of trees and shrubs, flailing his way through undergrowth, down, down towards the bay and the marina and the boat and Kamilah and escape. There was a roaring sound in his ears which he knew was either panic or low blood pressure—possibly both. How much blood had he lost? It felt like a lot but now he was also soaked with sweat so it was hard to tell if he was still bleeding.

Twice he had to cross a road, but it was now deep into the early hours and no traffic startled him. Working around the perimeters of other luxury properties was harder, as they had security lighting which he needed to keep low in the undergrowth to avoid. Stinging insects attacked him several times as he blundered through their world. At last he reached a rocky outcrop which dropped down to the sea. He was some way from the marina, which was on the far side of a jutting promontory. Could he swim to it? He was an excellent swimmer and he'd swum a mile or more through the sea to escape capture once before. He'd been bleeding then too, but nowhere near as much as he was bleeding now.

He must get to the boat, though. He must . . . He began to climb down the rocks, his lacerated palms and forearms making his head spin with pain as he forced them into use. When he reached the beach there were tears mingling with the blood on his face. He had never faced such horror as he had just lived through.

In the dim light from this quieter end of the

town Spook was just a shadow. In his black, blood-soaked clothes, he was hard to see. But he needed to be harder to see than this and he was too exhausted to maintain an illusory shield for long now. The exploding villa had sapped the last of his Cola strength. He spotted a shelf of rock close to the tide line and stumbled towards it. Beneath the shelf was a small cave—just big enough to scramble into. It stank of seaweed and dead fish. Spook didn't care. He struggled inside and pushed himself as far into its shelter as he could. If someone came very close and peered in with a torch they would find him, but nobody casually passing by would notice anything in the darkness. The rocks dug into his wounded skin and he began to shiver with delayed shock. But he felt marginally safer now and could at last allow his breathing to slow down while he tried to work out what to do next. He would rest for an hour and then attempt to cross the promontory and swim from the far side of it across to the marina where the boat was moored. Max, Kamilah, and Devlin would be looking out for him and would drag him aboard and set sail. The staff would tend his wounds and feed him and look after him and Kamilah would hang on every word of his appalling adventure and be so grateful that he had protected them all and made it back alive on his own. Focusing hard on this happy outcome, Spook felt his breathing slow and lengthen and at last he drifted into some kind of fitful sleep.

Fifty minutes later he realized sleep was no longer an option. He felt slightly rested but pain was pounding through him, across his throat and chest and arms and through his head. He guessed he was badly dehydrated—he needed to drink. Was he still losing blood? He eased out of the niche of rock, checking for signs of early beachcombers. Nobody was in sight. He gingerly patted his throat and found it sticky and lumpy, attempting to scab over but still dribbling blood. The wounds all over his chest and arms sent stabs of pain through him as he moved and he realized that many of them had welded to his shirt as the blood dried. Moving had ripped their silk scabs away and already he was bleeding afresh. But common sense now told him that he had not lost the vast amounts of blood he had at first imagined. He had probably sweated more than he had bled. Water. He needed water.

Squinting through the dim dawn light, Spook could make out a dark cleft in the rock face a few metres away from him, overhung by vegetation. He also thought he could hear trickling above the gentle, insistent sigh of the sea. He rose stiffly and made his way towards the sound, hoping for a freshwater stream. He was rewarded a few minutes later by cold water splashing thinly across his face and hands. He puffed out several gasps, but more with relief than shock at the cold. The water tasted good. He knew there were risks in drinking it but spring water was usually very pure, and at this stage filtered through much moss and vegetation. He filled his cupped hands and drank deeply, beginning to feel a little better. He splashed more water across the dog tooth puncture wounds on his arm and his throat, glad to feel the cleansing sting. Then he turned, scanned the area around him, and headed for the promontory. And as he walked he realized that maybe he would not need to swim across after all. If he had enough energy to swim, he certainly had enough to cloak himself in an illusion as he walked . . . that had to be the better option. He would walk.

He found the coast road a few minutes later

and began making his way along it. A car passed him soon after and while it passed he cloaked himself in simple shadow. This would be enough for anyone passing at speed in the dim light—and it was blissfully easy compared to all the tricks he'd needed last night. Streaks of pink and blue were spreading across the eastern sky as dawn rose. Spook checked his watch. It was 3.28a.m. He would be back in his luxurious bed by 5a.m. Clean and bandaged and able to sleep away the horrors he'd been through.

He guessed it was three or four kilometres to the marina. The kind of distance he could have jogged in twenty or thirty minutes in normal circumstances. But jogging was out of the question. Even walking a little faster brought about judders of pain through his chest, arms, and throat and made his head pound. The restorative water could only help so far.

By the time he was halfway (as far as he could judge) he was feeling lack of food too. He'd eaten very little of Bahkar's sumptuous dinner. His insides were growling now. A few minutes later a scent curled through the air which made his stomach give a plaintive whine. A *boulangerie*, he remembered dimly from his French lessons, starting early as they did here in France. Golden light and the delicious aroma of baked bread flooded out from the single storey building beside the road.

Cloaked in shadow, Spook eased up to the small window beside the wooden front door but it was steamed up and he couldn't see inside. The door, though opened halfway up, like a stable door, so he peered across that instead. Inside, two men dressed in floury white overalls were shoving metal trays filled with uncooked baguettes into a large oven. Freshly baked *pains au chocolat* lay in another tray on a scrubbed wooden table near the door. The sweet yeasty smell was agonizingly wonderful. Spook flicked his gaze to the far end of the room, conjured up another eye-catching rat, and watched the men slam the oven doors and then shout to each other and chase after the illusory rodent. He stepped into the room, silent in his battered suede-soled shoes, and scooped up as many *pains au chocolat* as he could carry.

They nestled warmly in his bloodstained arms as he moved on along the coast road in the growing dawn light. He counted five as he wolfed them down. The chocolate, still moist and dripping from the oven, gave him a surge of sugary energy while the flaky pastry soothed his angry belly.

After that he was able to walk faster and it was just after 4.45a.m. when he reached the marina. Quite a number of people were now about, so he focused on being dim. He had learned some time ago that remaining unnoticed didn't always require a full Cola illusion, just a dim wash of dullness which led people simply to filter out your presence. He applied this now and kept his distance from early sailors and service staff heading to work in shops and hotels.

Finally the berth he had last seen so many hours ago, before he'd become a high society thief, was within reach. He thumbed in the code on the panel at its security gate, pushed it open and walked on down the narrow wooden pontoon. The monstrous red catamaran the Sunseeker was moored next to hid his destination from view, but Spook's heart surged with delight as he realized he was home free at last. The anticipation of the comforts just a minute away now made him almost giddy and ecstatic. He didn't even care what he looked like. His wounds were badges of honour to wear in front of Kamilah.

Past the red cat he stood still. He blinked. His smile froze on his face.

The berth was empty.

18

For a while his brain simply refused to believe his eyes. The boat *had* to be there. It *had* to be.

And then adrenalin surged through him, sending darts of pain through his myriad wounds, and he turned and ran back and forth along the pontoon, frantically scanning all the berths, telling himself that he was too tired to remember where the Sunseeker lay. He *had* to be mistaken. He *had* to be.

But another part of his brain was telling him the truth. He had not wandered into a different part of the marina or along the wrong private pontoon. He had known the security code only to this pontoon and he knew perfectly well that Max's boat had been berthed alongside the huge red catamaran. And besides . . . the Sunseeker simply wasn't there.

There was no other yacht or motor cruiser here which he could fool himself into believing was Max's, shunted inexplicably along to a different position. There were several Sunseekers, true, but none of them of the same model as Max's.

He had to face it. Max and Kamilah and Devlin and the staff . . . they had weighed anchor and sailed away without him, leaving him to his fate. After all . . . they had the Van Gogh, didn't they? Why would they really need to wait? Spook felt a bitter twist in his insides and dropped to his knees beside the empty berth, retching. He vomited up all the pastry and chocolate and spring water into the dark water below, shaking and moaning and oblivious to anything but the horror of being abandoned.

And when at last he raised his head, wiping tears and blood and sweat from his eyes and nose, he saw several people coming towards the security gate at the end of the pontoon. Even in the dawn light he could see it was the gendarmerie. So . . . Bahkar had set the police on Max after all. Spook pulled dimness all around him but was so emptied out of energy and hope and spirit that he did not know whether even this patchy illusion would last.

It felt like fate as he tipped forward and flopped into the water.

He made very little splash, as close to it as he was, and he allowed himself to sink fully under, the cold water plunging into his ears almost a relief as it blotted out the world above. He gave two kicks to get away from the nasty drift of his ejected breakfast and then held fast to the nearest hull of the red catamaran. He pulled himself down under it and then rose again on its far side, into the wide air pocket between the twin hulls.

He could hear people walking along the pontoon; could see the ripples they made as they shook the floating jetty. He took several deep breaths, his heart now cold and much steadier, and then ducked beneath the water again, pulling himself under the second hull and gaining the far side of the catamaran a few seconds later. Now, he would swim.

Throwing a dark sea water illusion above his head and shoulders and across his shallow wake, Spook struck out from the marina and swam. In a few minutes he had left the pontoons far behind and was able to glance back at the three men standing next to Max's empty berth. Lights were on in the boats on either side; their occupants undoubtedly being questioned. *When had the boat left? Where was it heading?*

Spook swam south. After a few more minutes he realized that he had no idea where he was going. He also realized that he was too exhausted to go much further.

Idiot, said Gordon Williams in his head. *You set out again with no plan. When will you learn, Spencer? When will you ever learn?*

Spook's hands fluttered feebly in the water and his legs slowed down. He trod water for a while and tried to work out whether the dark shape coming towards him was a buoy or a dinghy or a whale. Maybe the whale was coming to swallow him up, like Jonah. God's punishment for his short burglary career. He found he was laughing, seawater flowing into his open mouth and choking him. The laughter went on regardless, spasming through his lacerated chest, even as he went under.

'SPOOK!'

Someone thumped him in the stomach.

'SPOOK!'

And rolled him fully over, pumping his arms, and back onto his back.

'SPOOK! BREATHE! DAMN YOU, SPOOK! BREATHE! BREATHE! BREATHE!'

Each demand was followed by a punch.

Spook felt his lungs contract like bellows and then water was churning up through his throat and out of his mouth. He gurgled and retched and groaned and felt air finally sucking back in. His head and body screamed with pain and his limbs and jaw shook uncontrollably. When hands grabbed his shoulders he swiped out feebly, sobbing with the overwhelming awfulness of it all. Then his mind clouded over and oblivion claimed him.

19

'Where are they?' Spook eased up on cotton pillows and stared at The Collector.

'Well,' he said, easing back into a curved wicker chair by the tall, low-silled window. 'That makes a change from "Where am I?".'

'I try to avoid cliché,' croaked Spook. Of course, he was desperate to know where he was too, but that could wait. He'd had a couple of hours after first drifting back to consciousness, to work out that he was not on Max's boat and not back at Fenton Lodge. He had woken alone in a room of modest proportions. It had thick, chocolate brown carpeting and its walls and vaulted ceiling were of tongue and groove pine, painted with a semi-opaque whitewash. A tall window opposite his bed offered a view which was most definitely *not*

Mediterranean. He was in a place which was set back only twenty metres or so from the edge of a cliff. A vast expanse of blue sea opened up beyond the cliff edge, narrowing, to the right of his view, to a cove, where it churned and boiled against black volcanic rocks. The green peninsular some three or four miles away on the far side revealed a tiny settlement of dwellings with steeply pitched slate roofs. Plumes of smoke from their chimneys blew almost flat inland. A wide silver stream ran past the settlement and then threw itself off the cliff in a twisting white waterfall. The view was starkly beautiful, but cold and obviously blasted by gales. There were no trees at all along the land; just a vast expanse of verdant turf, almost fluorescent beneath a low pearly sky.

Where am I? Spook had wondered to himself, before drifting back to a thin sleep where images of Kamilah and Bahkar and Dobermann hounds and his struggle across St Tropez bay whirled and spun and tried to make sense of themselves.

An hour or two later, he had rolled over and found water in a glass on a bedside table, beneath a paper-shaded lamp. His head hurt a little and his tongue was stuck to the top of his mouth, but other than that he felt rested and almost normal. He had quickly checked his chest wounds, beneath a clean white T-shirt, and discovered that they were merely red marks on his skin. His neck felt bruised . . . but there was no clotting bloody scab across the tear and no punctures on his arms or chest, either. Just more red marks, as far as he could see. Even his cast was gone; his left wrist looking a little pale and puny but otherwise normal.

How long had he been here?

Then he'd sensed a presence and glanced across to see The Collector, wearing black jeans and a grey sweater, sitting crossed-legged and barefooted in the wicker chair—and so he'd spoken his first three words.

'I would never accuse you of being clichéd,' smiled The Collector. 'You are a true original, Spook.'

'Did you pull me out of the sea?' asked Spook.

'I did,' said The Collector. 'And I pumped a fair bit of it out of your lungs. I can't believe you were giving up, Spook. Surely you weren't?'

Spook said nothing. Had he been giving up? Who, in his right mind, laughed himself into drowning? Only, of course, it hadn't really been laughter. It had been something else entirely.

'No matter, you're fine now,' said The Collector. 'Could you eat something?'

Spook nodded.

'Good,' said The Collector. 'I will be back with some soup and bread and we will talk. Properly, this time. Everything you want to know. I'll be back in ten minutes. Take a look at this while I'm gone.'

And he rose and handed Spook a paper-thin netbook. Spook opened it and rested it on his raised knees. The screen blinked out of sleep and showed him four camera feeds, in black and white but very clear. Spook frowned and peered hard at them for a few seconds before he recognized the views. They were rooms on the Sunseeker. Two were empty—his own room and the dining area of Max's room. Two others had occupants. Max and Devlin were in Max's cabin, talking earnestly on a couch beside the window. And in Kamilah's room, Kamilah lay on her bed, headphones over her ears, eyes closed, singing along to something. Even in black and white she looked fabulous, in another skimpy pale sundress, her hair loose and tumbling over the satin cushions behind her head and shoulders. Spook's mouth went dry and a hard pulse drummed his throat. He felt his insides squeeze tight, as if he was expecting a blow.

The Collector returned with soup and a large wedge of nutty brown bread, thickly spread with cold butter. He motioned Spook to sit up and deposited the tray across his knees as soon as Spook had shifted the netbook further down the bed.

'Eat,' he said, as Spook's eyes followed the screen. 'Then we can talk properly.'

Spook grabbed the buttered bread and dipped it into the soup, which appeared to be some thick chicken and vegetable broth. He returned the soup-dipped bread to his mouth and then found himself unable to stop eating until the bread and butter and soup were gone. He had been ravenously hungry. He barely noticed The Collector, back in his wicker chair, watching him throughout.

'Now,' he said, wiping his mouth with a cotton napkin from the tray and pointing to the netbook screen. 'Tell me. Where did they go?'

'They're in Italy,' said The Collector. 'They berthed this morning.'

'Why did they leave me behind?'

'Why would they stay?' asked The Collector.

'Because . . . because . . . I am apparently Max's

son . . . ?' Spook heard the whine in his voice and shut his mouth fast.

The Collector smiled. 'Yes, you would think that would be enough,' he agreed. 'Perhaps you failed to bond.'

'Failed to *bond*? What does *he* care? I was going to make him the best magician on the planet!'

'No you weren't, Spook,' said The Collector, shaking his head. 'At least, not for long. You were going to make *you* the best magician on the planet. Anyone could see that.'

'And Kamilah? She didn't care either?'

'Well . . . let's find out, shall we?' said The Collector, and he leaned across and pressed a button on the netbook, prompting an audio symbol and easing up the volume so Spook could hear the conversation between Max and Devlin.

' . . . two weeks, I think, before we'll hear anything,' said Max. He took a sip of something from a glass and went on, 'We need to let the dust settle, of course, but it looks as if a buyer is already lined up.' He raised the glass and Devlin mirrored him with a glass of his own. 'To a successful mission!'

'Successful?' spluttered Spook. The Collector said nothing.

'And a Van Gogh in the bilge tank!' laughed Devlin, chinking his glass to Max's. 'Any word on the boy?' he added.

Max looked a little uneasy, smoothing his hair and shaking his head. 'Bloody nuisance,' he said. 'I didn't think Bahkar would involve the police— Spook must have seriously aggravated him. It seems he staged some kind of explosion illusion after getting caught by the dogs. Of course, we only have Bahkar's word for it that he got away. They could be torturing him back in the villa's panic room now, for all we know.'

'Or, more likely, he's dead,' said Devlin, with a shake of ice cubes in his glass. 'Either way, we're in the clear. There's no proof that Spook wasn't working alone. The call from Bahkar was just an ego thing. He won't waste time chasing you.'

'It's a shame,' said Max. 'I was looking forward to much more from Spook. It's disappointing. Top up?' And he reached for a bottle.

Spook was speechless. *Disappointing?*

The Collector pulled a mobile phone from his pocket and dialled. A few seconds later the phone in Max's cabin shrilled out.

'It's TC,' grunted Max with a grimace, staring at

the phone. 'Damn . . . I'm not in the mood for this. That freak seriously gives me chills even when he's pleased with life—and he's not best pleased *now*, I'm betting.' He swiped up the phone. 'Hello— Max here.'

'Max,' said The Collector, silkily. 'I'm . . . ' he smiled knowingly at Spook, ' . . . not best pleased. You appear to have lost our prize.'

'Look—we've got the Van Gogh,' said Max. 'And there's a good chance Spook will catch up with us. Remember, he's a Cola. We shouldn't underestimate him.'

'We should not,' said The Collector. 'It seems, however, that I have very much *over*estimated *you*, Max.'

'Look,' said Max, getting to his feet and running his free hand through his hair again. 'I did everything you told me to do. I went along with every detail of your plan—I can't help it that it didn't go down exactly as we hoped. There was no choice but to get out of port. We waited an hour. And look at it this way—we're still £80 million better off, with or without Spook.'

'Your paternal concern is so touching,' said The Collector. 'And how does poor Kamilah feel?

No—don't tell me. Please—call her along to your room.'

Max held the phone away from him and motioned to Devlin. 'Go get Kamilah—The Collector wants a word.' Devlin departed and arrived, thirty seconds later, on the screen feed from Kamilah's room. While he urged her to take off her headphones and come with him, Max was continuing his conversation with The Collector, clearly unaware that he was being watched.

'Look—we've come out of this well,' he insisted. 'Bahkar has nothing to go on—Spook has vanished and the police say they have no further reason to pursue me. After all, the Van Gogh is back on the wall in Bahkar's gallery, as far as he knows, I've got a cast-iron alibi—and I'm out of French jurisdiction. They won't waste their resources coming after me.'

'So there's just the unfortunate loose end of your only son,' said The Collector. 'And you're an idiot if you think the Van Gogh is worth more than he is.'

Kamilah arrived now in the room. 'Is she there?' asked The Collector, knowing full well she was. 'Put her on.' Kamilah took the phone, looking nervous.

'I hear you made an excellent escape,' said The Collector. 'Too bad you left Spook behind.'

'I couldn't help it,' she said. 'I didn't know.'

'Of course not—you did the only thing you could,' said The Collector, soothingly. 'You played your role very well all round.'

Kamilah shrugged and said, 'I did what Max asked. It was no big deal.' She was shaking her head and shrugging at Max.

'Put me back on to Max,' said The Collector and she did, fast.

'We will talk again,' said The Collector. 'Just lie low for a few days. Do nothing to attract attention beyond your usual performances. I'll be in touch.' And he hung up.

Spook went to speak, filled with cold rage at Max, but The Collector waved him silent and pointed to the screen again where Max was returning the phone handset to its cradle and exhaling loudly.

'Well,' he said, pulling Kamilah into his arms. 'That could have been worse, baby.' And he kissed her. Kamilah wound her arms around his neck.

'No more play acting for you, anyway,' grinned Max, sliding his hands around her waist. 'Will you miss your toyboy?'

Kamilah laughed and stared up at Max with a doe-eyed expression. 'Ooooh, Spook!' she breathed. 'You are *so* amazing! You make me a little scared . . . '

Spook felt sick. The Collector touched his shoulder and let his hand remain there, lightly. The sickness ebbed away, to be replaced by cold fury.

'Well, I won't miss the babysitting,' said Kamilah, sitting down on the couch and examining her nails. 'Or that insufferable smugness. Or the sweaty hand-holding and the dribbly kisses . . . eeurgh! It was like being nuzzled by an over-excited spaniel.'

Max pulled her along to sit on his lap and said, 'You did good, baby.'

Spook slammed the netbook shut.

'Yes,' said The Collector. 'I think we've seen all we need to.'

'It was all a set up,' said Spook. There was no question in his voice.

'Yes,' said The Collector. 'And I had my part to play in that, I confess.'

Spook looked at him, sharply, and The Collector held his gaze with eyes bluer than the cold sea behind him. 'I did think that Max's world could be a good starting point for you—somewhere to make the transition from being a Cola captive for a year or two,' said the man. 'But I wasn't sure about his . . . character. I could see flaws. Weakness. The only way to find out was to guide him towards the heist plan and see how he managed it . . . how much concern he spent on you. And the answer is, of course, precious little.'

'And you still think he's my father?'

The Collector dipped his head and made a rueful face. 'I very much wish I could tell you that he wasn't . . . but he is.'

Spook gritted his teeth. To be a blood relative of a low-life like Max Carlyle was a bitter pill to swallow.

'You feel angry,' said The Collector. 'And why wouldn't you? *I* feel angry and it wasn't even me they betrayed. I am furious at their stupidity. Do you know what my best hope was, Spook? That Max would refuse to allow the heist to go ahead; that he would tell me you were too precious to risk.'

Spook said nothing, but concentrated on the furious sea doing battle with the black rocks.

'Of course, I can even the score with Max at any time,' said The Collector, flipping the netbook back open and rattling his fingers across the keys.

Spook glanced back at the screen and saw that an email had been opened on it, across the live feed which still showed Max and Kamilah wrapped around each other on the couch.

'This email carries an attachment with all the information needed for the Italian police to seize the boat and find the Van Gogh,' said The Collector. 'There is not a shred of evidence which will ever lead to me—but easily enough information to help them lock Max away for years. And when he gets out, of course, his career will be over; he'll be penniless and homeless. Even the boat I gave him will be confiscated.'

'Don't you want your share of the £80 million?' asked Spook. The Collector merely shrugged.

'And Kamilah?' Spook queried, as Max played with Kamilah's hair.

'Oh, well, she has quite a history herself,' smiled The Collector. 'Many unsavoury sidelines, including drug smuggling. She'll most likely be deported to her homeland to answer for earlier offences. She was born in Turkey—she'll do her time there. Ten, maybe fifteen years. Turkish jails, as you probably know, are brutal. I imagine she'll come out a lot less pretty.'

Spook stared at The Collector's fingers hovering over the cursor pad. A little arrow moved towards the email. 'It can't be traced back to me,' said The Collector. 'Officially, I don't exist. So . . . what do you think, Spook? You choose. To email or not to email? That is the question.'

Spook knocked the man's fingers aside. And hit SEND.

20

'The Faroe Islands.' The Collector shielded his eyes from the morning sun and gazed across the ragged rocks below them. 'North of the Hebrides. Danish people with a big British influence.'

'Why are you here?' asked Spook. He clambered down the sloping cliff, disturbing a nearby huddle of puffins, and sat down on a smooth lump of ancient volcanic matter.

'Here on the Faroes? Or here in your life?' said The Collector, finding a seat nearby and turning a quizzical blue stare on Spook. 'Here on the Faroes because I like it and it's easy to stay under the world's radar here. I can't be dowsed here either—and nor can you, while you're with me. I travel a lot, Spook, but this is the only place I call home.'

'OK,' said Spook, still regarding him warily. 'So what brings you into my life, Collector?'

The man smiled and let his attention drift out across the sea. It was calmer today and a small sandy beach had been exposed by the ebbing tide, six or seven metres below their perch. There were a couple of children playing on it, with a dog. 'I can't explain it *all* to you now, Spook—but know this—I am here *for you*. For every Cola who will one day need me. And trust me on this, Spook, you *will* need me. Many of you.'

'Many of us?'

He looked back at Spook again, his face serious. 'But you first, Spook. Above all, Spook, *you*.'

Spook shook his head. 'Can't you ever just make sense? It's like the name, isn't it? Don't you have a real name? What the hell does *The Collector* mean?'

'It's very simple,' said The Collector. 'It's what I am. I am able to collect certain abilities from people. If I spend any time with someone who speaks Greek, I will quickly pick up Greek. Collect it. I may not remember it for ever, but for as long as I need it, I have it, collected inside me. I collect talent too—I played concert piano before an audience of thousands two weeks after sharing a flight with the London Symphony Orchestra. I have flown a helicopter just an hour after getting inside one for the first time, thanks to the very able pilot I collected from. I hacked into the Pentagon last summer, after a couple of beers with an IT genius. I am a collector. It's what I do.'

Spook stared at him, excitement, recognition, and deep unease battling inside him. 'You're like Catherine,' he said, at last. 'Like Gideon and Luke Reader's sister. She was a parasite too.'

'Parasite is a little harsh,' chuckled The Collector. 'I don't kill or injure the people I collect from. I've saved many lives through my collecting. Catherine, you have to remember, grew up unchecked and unsupervised, around people who knew nothing of her talents. She never learned when to stop taking. It was always going to end badly. Very sad, her death.'

'Not for us, it wasn't,' muttered Spook. 'She nearly killed me.' He still winced every time he remembered his last encounter with Catherine. Then another thought occurred to him—a more important one.

'Are you telling me you're . . . some kind of Cola too?'

The Collector leaned his elbows onto his knees and tilted his head at Spook. 'Not exactly, Spook,' he said. 'There have always been people on this planet with extraordinary talents—for centuries—but most of them either die at the hands of the people they've terrified or learn, very fast, to cloak their powers and survive. I'm not saying they have been as powerful as *you*... I do think the Colas are something completely new. But I am certain you are not the first alien half-breeds to have shown up on Earth.'

'And you're one of those?' asked Spook. 'Half alien—like us?'

'Possibly,' shrugged The Collector. 'I never knew either of my parents and no government ever plucked me out of my childhood in order to study, control and use me. I managed to hide my powers from a very young age. I use them all the time, of course, but I generally manage to convince people that I am . . . extra-ordinary, rather than extra-terrestrial.'

'How did you find out about me? About all of us?' asked Spook.

'Aaah, well you see, I used to work for the UK government,' he said. 'In intelligence, among other things. So when word eventually leaked out about the Cola Project, I got to hear about it. I am . . . very well connected.' He stood up and gazed out to sea with some kind of emotion washing his face which Spook could not easily read. 'It was astonishing to think that I was not alone. And soon I found myself wondering how the people who would take care of you could possibly understand your needs.'

'Paulina Sartre is talented too,' pointed out Spook. 'Our principal—she is a seer and a dowser, like Lisa.'

'Nothing like Lisa,' corrected The Collector. 'Lisa's powers already completely dwarf Paulina's and she knows it. All of you in the True Eleven . . . you're already filling your own people with terror. They're very scared. Had you not noticed?'

Spook said nothing. It was something he did not like to dwell on.

'But I'm *not*,' concluded the man, turning and making his way back up the rocks. 'I am not scared of you. Not of any of you. And that is why you will need me.'

Spook followed him, climbing up the slope on legs which still felt a little weak.

'Why don't you offer your services to the Cola Project, then?' he asked.

The Collector laughed loudly, throwing his head back and revealing even white teeth. 'Ooooh, I don't think so, Spook. I've never been able to work as part of a team. Especially as frightened a team as the Cola Project. I need my freedom to help you get yours, Spook.'

'So . . . what do we do next?' asked Spook, standing still on the cliff top and staring at The Collector. 'What's the plan?'

The man turned, dropped the smile and simply rested his intense blue stare on the boy for a few seconds. When he stepped forward and rested his hands on Spook's shoulders, Spook felt an unfamiliar sense of security wash over him. It brought a lump to his throat.

'There is a plan. I can tell you part of it today, but tomorrow you must be gone.'

'Gone?' Spook exhaled sharply. Dear God, was he ever going to stop anywhere long enough to get his bearings?

'Yes—back to Fenton Lodge.'

Spook was speechless. He simply stared at the man, shaking his head.

'You cannot stay with me, here. Not yet.' The Collector looked as if he was genuinely sad to say this. 'As much as I would love it . . . and truly, Spook, I would. You belong here—alongside me. One day soon, that's where you'll be. Exactly as you should be. But the time is not right now. Furthermore, I will need you to bring others to me. Your fellow Colas think they are tied for ever to your government and the lives of endless servitude which are carefully planned for you all. This is no longer the only option. I can offer other choices. So—I need you back there, helping me. Then, when you come to me as my right-hand man, your life will properly begin.'

Spook turned away and let his eyes drift back down to the beach to the children and the dog. He thought of his half brother and sister. When did he ever see them anyway? Twice a year? Summer holidays and Christmas? And they were more awkward with him every time. His father . . . well, in name, anyway . . . had disconnected from him a long time ago and his stepmother, although kind, really did not understand him; feared him even, a little, when he was around her children.

He had not ever felt as if he belonged. In his early schools he was not rich enough. In Cola Club he was not liked enough. He turned back and raised his eyes to The Collector's and pinpricks of *knowing* ran across his skin. Here was his answer.

'Come,' said The Collector, putting a warm arm around his shoulders and guiding him back to the house. 'Let's have fish and chips for lunch.'

Lunch, in a hexagonal dining room of more whitewashed wood and high windows on stunning sea views, was utterly filling. His mind was filled more, even, than his belly. By the time the plates were cleared by a quiet grey-haired lady and they were left alone with glasses of chilled lemonade, Spook was grinning with delight at The Collector's amazing ideas and audacious plans. Then his grin subsided.

'There is a problem,' he said. 'Fenton Lodge has mind readers. Some of them quite good,' he added, thinking of Lisa. 'If I show up again, pretending to have amnesia or something, they're just going to line up the mind readers and they'll go through my head like a swarm of locusts.'

'And they'll find nothing,' said The Collector.

'How? How will they find nothing?' demanded Spook. 'You might be able to protect me from

224

dowsing, from miles and miles away, but mind-reading's different. They'll be right in my face!'

'They'll find nothing because there will *be* nothing,' said The Collector. 'Until the time is right, your mind must be wiped clean.' He got to his feet, placing his linen napkin on the table and walking towards Spook's chair.

'Oh, come *on,*' said Spook.

'I wish I had longer with you,' said The Collector. 'And I really wish this wasn't going to hurt so much.'

'What do you mean, "hurt so much"?' Spook felt a sharp sting of fear shoot right through him as he saw the expression on The Collector's face. His features were smooth . . . almost glassy . . . and his blue eyes seemed to have a flare of white light inside each pupil. 'What do you mean?' he asked, again, and the fear was riding his voice now, making him whine like a child.

'I have to hypnotize you—to prepare your mind.'

'Why should that hurt?' breathed Spook, gripping the arms of the chair in a spasm of terror.

'It doesn't. It's what must happen first. Before I can implant the hypnosis this deep in your mind . . . I have to break your mind.'

The Collector stepped behind Spook's chair.

'Wait! Wait!' yelled Spook, a feeling of terrifying dread now engulfing him.

The Collector put his hands on Spook's head.

Two seconds later Spook began to scream.

21

A corrugated cardboard cup sat in his hands but the hot drink inside it—tea, he thought . . . tea?—had long since gone cold. He stared into the beige disc of liquid and then moved his eyes, for what felt like the first time, to the table he was leaning on. It was orange—some kind of plastic topped thing. Cheap. Smeared. Not very clean.

Noise suddenly flooded into his ears, making him jerk upright in his seat. The babble of people and traffic, along with the smell of burgers and chips and ketchup, assaulted his senses and made his heart pound. Where was he? What was this? Where was he? Where was he? Who was he?

He could see cars through the glass doors to his right and small shops beside this café. The word MOTO large on a sign.

There was a piece of paper creased up in his left fist. As he unclenched his palm it fell onto the table top and he opened it up with slow fingers. On it were some words written in black ink, the letters smooth and forward-sloping. *'Your name is Spook Williams. You must call Control on the number below immediately. There are coins in your pocket and a pay phone is to your left. Call the number and then swallow this piece of paper.'*

Spook obeyed the words, moving in an odd shuffle to the phone and slowly punching the numbers into it. As soon as he spoke his name to this 'Control' person his world seemed to speed up. They found him very soon, still holding the receiver and staring numbly at it while the voice on the other end reassured him and told him not to move. The note was long swallowed.

Three men came to get him; two well-built and wearing casual clothes, looking around the crowds intently as they moved, and one in a dark suit, wearing rimless spectacles and an expression of great concern, who called himself Chambers.

'Do you know me?' he asked, his brows drawn down as he touched Spook's shoulder and stared intently into his eyes.

'I am Spook Williams,' said Spook. And those four words were all he said for the next forty-eight hours.

It was nearly a week before he properly remembered who he was. Or used to be. In that time he stayed in the medical room with Janey, the Fenton Lodge doctor, while a series of people came to see him and check him over. He felt calm; had felt calm ever since he had obeyed the note.

There were bruises and scars on him and a hairline fracture in his left wrist—but no serious damage. Janey spoke of 'shock' and 'trauma' but he didn't feel shocked or traumatized. He felt fine. They were worried, anyway.

They brought Mia to him quite early on. He recognized her immediately.

Her lovely violet eyes were wide when she looked at him. Her hands sent waves of healing warmth all through his body. It was very agreeable but it didn't seem to stop them worrying. Mia stayed until she was aching and tearful and they had to make her leave. It occurred to Spook that Mia might love him. How funny was that?

As his senses returned he felt calmer than he had ever felt . . . as far as he could remember. And that was the point, really. He couldn't remember; not anything since leaving Fenton Lodge with Darren for the hospital trip. He had been gone for ten days, they told him. Ten days filled with intense high level military and Cola Project activity as his country desperately tried to retrieve him.

And then, when he told them he could remember nothing, they sent for Lisa. Who else? None but the very best. Darren came with her, looking wan and tired himself. He'd broken his nose and jaw in this coach crash they were all going on about, and had suffered internal bleeding. He had been raced back to Fenton Lodge where Mia saved his life. He told Spook this in a panicky rush, as if trying to distract himself from the sight of his best friend. Spook realised there was something in his eyes they weren't comfortable with. He had no idea what. In the mirror he looked just the same, if a little thinner.

'Shut up now, Darren,' said Lisa, taking Spook's hand with a slight grimace. She made no secret of how she felt about Spook.

She was rummaging around in his head for half an hour while he lay back on the lavender scented pillows and waited, with interest, for what she might find. Eventually, sulky and defeated, she had to tell Chambers what she'd found.

Nothing. As far as the past ten days were concerned there was nothing at all.

Collected

Dax Jones was in the tree house when Spook climbed into it two weeks later on a quiet afternoon after lessons. Darren was coming to join him but had gone up to their room for his binoculars.

'Oh joy,' sneered Spook. 'I thought I could smell something rank. Can't you go off and chew a rabbit somewhere?'

Dax stayed in fox form and stared at Spook for a few seconds. Then he morphed into a boy, sitting cross-legged on the platform, eyeing his least favourite fellow student with fascination. 'You're back to your old self then,' he said. 'Remembered any of your missing life yet?'

'I wouldn't tell *you* if I did,' said Spook, sitting on one of the little wooden stools at the far end of the tree house platform.

'They say it's trauma,' said Dax. 'Something bad happened. What do you reckon?'

Spook shrugged. 'I refer you to my previous answer,' he said.

Dax grinned and raised a dark eyebrow. 'You might have done something *really* embarrassing and had to block it out. Maybe you were forced to wear baggy jeans from Primark. Maybe it rained and your hair went frizzy in public and you had a panic attack.'

'Well, you'd know all about panic attacks, wouldn't you?' snipped back Spook. 'Had any run-ins with hunting dogs late—' The words suddenly strangled in his throat. He felt his heart rate shoot up and saw blazes of red stars shoot across his vision. The white-hot blast of panic brought with it a terrible vision of slavering jaws. He cried out and reached impulsively for his throat.

'What? Spook—what is it?' Jones was sounding concerned now, as if he was a friend. Spook didn't speak—he just screwed up his eyes and got control of his breathing. His memory had just returned and it was like being hit by a truck. The events of his lost days hurtled back into his brain and all the emotions he had experienced hit him in quick succession. Fear and confusion and lust and joy and triumph and horror and abandonment and . . . and . . .

'I'm getting Janey,' he heard Dax say and then felt the downdraught of a wing as the boy flew away.

But after thirty seconds Spook was in control again. The last memory he had been left following his adventures was of The Collector, telling him how to lock everything back down again as soon as he recalled it.

'I will take you deep enough to bury your memory for at least two weeks,' said The Collector, sitting on the windowsill with the cliffs and sea framed in the glass behind him. 'Time enough for the pressure to be off you; for the mind probing to let up; for you to get back to your old self.' He looked blurry. Spook's eyes had been filled with tears after the terrible pain of the first strike inside his head.

'Then you will go to the tree house and your memory will return. You will understand *everything* and start to prepare for what lies ahead. Any time you need to switch your memory off you can do so by touching your temples and blinking three times. This will cut out your memory of these days for twelve hours, leaving nothing for Lisa or any other mind reader to find. And when it returns, you can carry on, planning for me. Waiting for my next instruction. We'll begin, I think, with Mia.

'Thank you, Spook. It won't be long now . . . '

Half an hour later Lisa was brought to him again, down in the development level in the basement. She was not keen.

'All I've got the last three times is a really unpleasant insight into Spook Williams's inner thoughts,' she complained. 'I really don't want to spend any more time in his smug little head.'

'I have to agree,' Spook told Chambers. 'This is a waste of time. I don't care what Dax Jones told you—I just had a coughing fit, that's all. I can't remember anything new.'

Chambers gave him a tight smile. 'Nevertheless, Spook, we're going to try again. Don't you *want* to know what happened to you?'

Spook shrugged and shook his head. 'Well . . . I suppose so,' he sighed. He pressed his fingers to his temples. 'Give it another try, Hardman,' he sighed. And blinked three times.

Twenty minutes later they hadn't got much further.

'Nothing!' snapped Lisa, now in a severely bad mood, much to Spook's amusement.

'We could try Mia again,' he said, with a bright smile. 'Just to get me nice and relaxed. She always reaches the parts you can't,' he added, just to wind Lisa up more. And a bit more Mia time would certainly be good . . . And why shouldn't he feel good? Even when Mia cried he felt good.

'I got *one* thing,' said Lisa, narrowing her eyes at him in contempt. 'But it doesn't mean anything.'

'What?' said Chambers.

'It's only one word,' she shrugged. 'No help at all.'

'Lisa!' said Chambers, his voice terse. 'What word? Tell me.'

Lisa walked towards the door, and called over her shoulder.

'Collected.'

Ali Sparkes is a journalist and BBC broadcaster who chucked in the safe job to go dangerously freelance and try her hand at writing comedy scripts. Her first venture was as a comedy columnist on *Woman's Hour* and later on *Home Truths*. Not long after, she discovered her real love was writing children's fiction.

Ali grew up adoring adventure stories about kids who mess about in the woods and still likes to mess about in the woods herself whenever possible. She lives with her husband and two sons in Southhampton, England. Check out www.alisparkes.com for the latest news on Ali's forthcoming books.

UNLEASHED

SPEAK EVIL
JANUARY 2014

'Waddayareckon?' asked Jacob.

Alex put a toe into the clear water and abruptly pulled it out again. 'Cold!' he shivered.

Jacob grimaced. It looked inviting, but despite the summer sun he knew their favourite pool was fed by streams from high up in the fells. Even in summer it was not going to be warm.

'Come on!' Alex was already stripping down to blue trunks and goose bumps.

'Mmmmm. Not sure.' Jacob eyed the grassy bank and thought about sunbathing instead. He had his iPod with him. Lazing was looking like a better option.

'Come on! It was your idea!' Alex, pulling goggles over his eyes, stepped in up to his knees and let out a little song of shock. 'D-don't wimp out on me!' The goose bumps were mountainous now.

Jacob grinned and shook his head. 'Nah—it'll be more fun lounging on the bank, listening to your whimpers.'

'Death or glory!' yelled Alex and plunged in head first. He went right under, with an upward flip of his feet, like a dolphin's tail. Alex's shout, as his whole body was submerged, was loud in Jacob's head, but not his ears. His brother couldn't actually shout with his face underwater.

So—how is it down there? Jacob asked, grinning as he settled on the bank, his palms behind his head. Bracing?

Like a Slush Puppy, Alex gurgled back. Freeeeezing. You should come in! Ooooh—trout! Just saw a trout! Come IN!

In a while, sent back his brother, putting his earbuds in and spooling through his album selection screen.

Another trout . . . and . . . tench, I think, went

on Alex. He surfaced briefly, took a gasp of air and ducked down again. The pool was smaller than the lake up beside Fenton Lodge. Other kids from the college came down here sometimes, but not often. Usually Jacob and Alex had it to themselves. They had a perfectly good indoor swimming pool too, and they used it a lot, but the pool down here was special. They felt it was theirs.

More trout . . . sent Alex.

Jacob sighed. Sometimes the gift of telepathy could be irritating. OK—enough of the underwater commentary now, he sent back, Unless you spot a shark! Or a portal to another dimension . . . He settled back to listen to 'Sir Duke', happily playing air bass guitar along with it with his eyes closed.

Look, said Alex, his head bobbing up and then going back under halfway across the pool, if I can't tell you about my new fishy friends, can you stop channelling Stevie Wonder? It doesn't work in my underwater world . . .

Jacob turned down the volume on their telepathic link. He could not explain how this was possible—nor could Alex. They'd both been asked to explain this and many other aspects of their Cola talent for telepathy, by the scientists who ran the Development sessions. All kinds of tests had measured the scope of their talent, establishing that while their brother-to-brother link was easy and instinctive; connecting telepathically with others was trickier. Harder work.

Some people were easy to communicate with—like Lisa and most of the psychic mediums. Assuming they wanted to be communicated with. Those with similar talents had learned some time ago how to block other telepaths. Dax Jones, the only Cola who could shapeshift, was also able to pick up their communications, but sometimes not the detail—his form of telepathy was like an animal's. After all, he was part-time animal. Top telepaths like Lisa could reach him quite easily, but even she usually needed to make some kind of contact first.

Jacob and Alex had found, though, that even ordinary people could be communicated with on some level, once you'd made eye contact or grabbed their hand or something. They didn't realize it, of course—and they rarely got all the detail—but you could definitely plant ideas in their heads. He and Alex were always planting the idea, with the kitchen staff, that they should get extra cake or biscuits. Mrs Polgammon, head of catering, had only recently worked out what they were doing. Probably one of the teachers had tipped her off.

At the far end of the pool now, Alex rose, flipped over onto his back and floated lazily under the warmth of the sun. Now that he'd adjusted to the cold water he felt fantastic—invigorated. But he didn't bother to convince his brother to join him. Jacob was lost in his music now.

Alex let the cool water lap into his ears as he floated, submerged to his temples. Occasionally he turned and dipped beneath the surface where the sun streamed through in shafts of greenish gold, lighting up an amazing world filled with fish and frogs, and then bobbed back up to float on his back again. It was nearly 4 p.m. The day's lessons were over and tea was only an hour away. He flapped his feet, propelling himself along gently. Good times, he thought.

Jacob had reached one of his favourite tracks. He turned it up super loud and closed his eyes again to concentrate.

The explosion, when it came, nearly passed him by.

Alex could not believe what he was witnessing.

A huge fountain of water was hurling itself up and out, its shock waves rocking him violently in the pool. And something was emerging out of it— shooting back up with as much velocity as it had entered the water. Sparkling droplets flew in every direction, glinting like diamonds in the sun, as a head and two hands erupted from the lake. The eyes were dark, wide and shocked——and one of the hands reached out and grabbed his foot.

'HOME!' gasped the face.

And Alex felt the lake remove itself from his life.